Beached

and other stories

Scottish Arts Trust Story Awards
Volume Four
2022

Edited by
Sara Cameron McBean
and Claire Rocha

Scottish Arts Trust

Other publications from the Scottish Arts Trust

The Desperation Game and other stories from the Scottish Arts Trust Story Awards 2014-2018 (Volume 1). Edited by Sara Cameron McBean and Hilary Munro (2019)

Life on the Margins and other stories from the Scottish Arts Trust Story Awards 2019-2020 (Volume 2). Edited by Sara Cameron McBean and Michael Hamish Glen (2020)

A Meal for the Man in Tails and other stories from the Scottish Arts Club Story Awards 2021 (Volume 3). Edited by Sara Cameron McBean and Michael Hamish Glen (2021)

Rosalka: The Silkie Woman and other stories, plays and poems by Isobel Lodge (2018)

———

Writing Awards at the Scottish Arts Trust

Enter our writing competitions through our website at
www.scottishartstrust.org

Short Stories

First prize £3,000: The Scottish Arts Club Short Story Competition is
open to writers worldwide and stories on any topic up to 2,000
words. Enter from 1 December to 28 February.

First prize £750: The Isobel Lodge Award is for the top short story
entered in the competition by an unpublished writer living in
Scotland.

First Prize: £300: The Write Mango Award – for the top short story
that is fun, amusing, bizarre and as delicious as a mango!

Flash Fiction

First prize £2,000: The Edinburgh Award for Flash Fiction is open to
writers worldwide and stories on any topic up to 250 words. Enter
from 1 June to 31 August.

First Prize £500: The Golden Hare Award is for the top flash fiction
entry by a writer living in Scotland, published or unpublished.

Authors of at least 20 leading entries from the short story and flash
fiction competitions are offered publication in our next anthology.

Contents

Dirty Pictures by Mandy Wheeler 9

They will come no more… by Sheena Cook 16

The Witch by David Butler 22

Evening in the Tropics by Mike Lunan 28

The Letter from the Home Office by Gail Anderson 31

Sea Fret by Kathy Hoyle 32

Things visible and invisible by Michael Callaghan 33

Taenia Saginata's Last Words by Andrew Gardiner 35

Three Fish Suppers by Lyn Irving 36

A Lesson on Conditionals by Kirsty Hammond 42

Vibrating at the Speed of Light by David Martin 43

How to Draw a Frog by Bruce Meyer 49

The Art of Convenience by Ann Seed 50

Silence by Frances Sloan 57

A Prayer Unanswered by David Francis 58

Unmute by Cath Staincliffe 59

Please connect with me… by Katy Lennon 66

Forked Tongue by Hazel Osmond 68

Mona Lisa by Ann Frost 69

Blockdown by Ann Seed 70

Chinese Whispers by Shannon Savvas 72

The sugarless sweet pudding by Gayathiri Dhevi Appathurai 78

Nothing says Christmas like Tinsel by Cindy Bennet 79

The Hill by David Simmonds 84

The old woman by the fish tank by Keith McKibbin 85

The Lucky Man by Ishbel Smith...91

Nuisance Calls by Eva Sneddon...92

Blind Love by Louise Mangos...93

Lipstick by Amy Macrae 99

Spaceship Head by Karen Storey 100

The Bench by Lynsey Clark...106

The lonely man by Tim Roelandt 113

A Love Letter by Sarah Brown 114

Green Dreams by Edith Reznák 121

Stella by Jessica Redfern..122

Angie by Eric O'Callaghan...127

43 Milliken Lane by Julie Adams 128

You by Margaret Callaghan 131

A Shortcut to Nowhere by Ewan Gault..133

Just a walk in the Park by Macleay Lindsay..................................139

The Last Tram by Frank Carter 141

Seas the Day by Ann Seed 147

Crescendo by Ken Cohen 148

The Sound of Music by Andy Raffan 154

The Two Gems by Kate Blackadder 155

The Disappearing by Hilary Plews 156

Double Espresso by Sally Arkinstall 163

In Hope of Bread by Caroline Kohl 164

Final Rinse by Andrew Gardiner 170

Leaf by Jane Pearn...171

The Crinkle and the Crumb by Julie Dron 175

Condition: *Spinster* by Michael Toolan..176

Returning by Jane Broughton 182

Achill by Chris Lee 183

Wormhole by Etienne Essery 189

The Last Puppet by Catherine Ogston 190

Why they like to lie by Ros Thomas 195

Down with the Doubles by Lorraine Queen 197

Gulag by Orla Murphy 198

If there had been phones by Ann Seed 205

The Unfinished Room by Caoimhe O'Leary 206

Still goin' strong by Heather Finlayson 212

Beached by Lorraine Queen 214

The Scottish Arts Trust Story Awards 215

Acknowledgements 217

Dirty Pictures
by Mandy Wheeler

Winner, Scottish Arts Club Short Story Competition 2022

*T*o fully understand the impact of 'V' you need to remember when it was painted. Back in the 1960s the vagina was a mystery; even to many of those who had one. To those who didn't, it was something like the USSR; they'd heard a lot about it, but unless they'd actually visited, they had no idea what went on there, over the border, under the panty line.

It was into this social climate that 'V' was launched in 1967. The rest, as they say, is art history.

(Extract: *'Age Cannot Wither Her: Revisiting Merion Taylor's 'V'*. Catalogue essay for 'Dirty Pictures?', Tate Modern 2016).

'Start at the beginning.'

'Way back there?'

'If you don't mind.'

'I'll do my best. I was 23... no, I was 24. I met Merion at a gallery, a private view, something like that. Bond St, Chelsea, I don't know. I would have been with my aunt. She was on a mission to stop me becoming a teacher — to stop me becoming too square. She lived in a squat in Stoke Newington with a bunch of other artists. I don't remember what she made — pottery, I think. She certainly smoked a lot of dope.'

'I remember I was wearing some kind of tie-dye shift dress. Orange or purple. Everything was orange or purple back then. Except Merion of course, he was always in black — black leather waistcoat, black frock coat and that long black ponytail. Do you remember the ponytail? No, you're too young. But you've seen pictures. He was pretty gorgeous you know, if you liked that kind of thing. And he was so thin. That was the drugs.'

Over the years since its famous unveiling at Marshall Hampton's gallery, the question has been asked many times: Is 'V' a great painting or

9

just a product of its time? Was Merion Taylor a talented artist, or simply an attention seeking bad boy who mesmerised the art market at time when politicians were lining up to be photographed with East End gangsters?

Plenty of cultural commentators — not to mention artists and writers, media studies professors and feminists — have been kept busy debating 'V' over the last five decades. Was it truly transformative or merely transgressive? Does Taylor have any place in the art history canon, or should he simply be remembered a crowd-pleasing self-publicist?

In other words — was Merion Taylor's 'V' just a dirty picture?
(Extract: *'Age Cannot Wither Her: Revisiting Merion Taylor's V'*.
Catalogue essay for 'Dirty Pictures?', Tate Modern 2016).

'He painted 'V' in Amsterdam?'

'Yes. We flew out the morning after we met. I was still wearing the shift dress. Orange or purple, I don't remember.'

'What did you do in Amsterdam?'

'What did we do?? How old are you, for Christ's sake?'

'I mean 'V', how —?'

'We were in bed — he propped the canvas up against the pillows. The bed was right under the window. We could hear people partying on the canal all night. It was hot that summer, hot and sticky...'

'People have remarked that you look like a woman who's just...'

'You don't say.'

'I'm sorry, I didn't mean to — '

'I didn't know he was going to sell it, you know. I didn't even think he was going to show anyone. That's how stupid I was.'

Daily Mirror March 1967
'FILTH!!'

The tide of depravity that is the 'permissive society' threatened to engulf the West End last night. A mere three miles from Buckingham Palace, the so called 'artist' Merion Taylor opened his latest show in Mayfair. In a theatrical flourish, Mr Taylor, who arrived on a white horse and dressed in a black frock coat, drew back a red silk curtain to reveal the centrepiece of his exhibition, a new painting that Mr Taylor calls 'V'. This latest offering, heralded by the trendy art set as 'ground-breaking', is an image is of such explicit detail that we would never show it in a decent family newspaper such as this one. We can assure you though, it is FILTH of the highest order. What, oh what, is happening to this country?

(An edited version of the image is reproduced on page three, along with the address of the gallery where the work is currently on show. Entrance is free.)

'I never saw Merion again after Amsterdam. He told me on the plane coming back that he was married. That was a smart move — you can't storm off an aeroplane. I left him at the airport. I went home to Nottingham and got a teaching job. Forgot all about Merion. Thought that was the end of it.'

'Then he pulled that ridiculous unveiling stunt. You know he kicked off a bidding war right there in the gallery? Some sleazy American property developer bought 'V', took it to his yacht and snorted coke off it.'

'You were voted the face of 1967—'

'It wasn't my face they were interested in. The papers blacked out the part that people really wanted to see.'

BBC News March 1972

Today at Sotheby's New York, the infamous painting 'V' by the enfant terrible of British art, Merion Taylor, was on show again. Last seen in London in the late 60s, the painting was in the collection of the US playboy Michael Clarke until it was seized by the US government following Clarke's conviction for tax evasion.

In 1970 Taylor famously attempted to buy the painting back claiming Clarke had mistreated the artwork by using it as a tabletop in his yacht. The painting, which has been subject to extensive cleaning since the discovery of Class A drugs on its surface, is expected to reach a record price for a work of this period.

'You know how much his paintings used to sell for? It was crazy. Most of the idiots who bought his stuff didn't care a toss about art — they just wanted a piece of Merion. He was a celebrity.'

'The papers made sure everyone was talking about 'V'. Even the Archbishop of Canterbury got involved. I lost my job. Didn't have a hope of getting another one. Oh, I got offered plenty of glamour modelling, but no school would touch me. People pointed at me in the street. So, I went away.'

'To?'

'Nowhere.'

Venice Biennale Catalogue 1979
24: **The Green (Wo) Man**
Installation piece. A three-dimensional reinterpretation of 'V' by Merion Taylor. (Mixed media: Box hedge and paper clips).

'Nowhere?'

'Just shut the doors and stayed home. Dyed my hair, put on weight, got old. That's how I disappeared, by getting old. And, of course, I changed my name.'

'You were 29.'

'Not me. 'V' was the young and beautiful one. She had my life. And I believe she had quite a good time with it — she certainly got around.'

Edinburgh Festival Fringe 1983.
Assembly Rooms. 10.30pm daily.
'Intimate conversations'
Performance piece in which genitalia from well-known art pieces (including Merion Taylor's 'V' and Michelangelo's 'David') debate representation vs exploitation. Over 18s only. Contains puppets.

'Is that everything?'

'Everything I can remember.'

'It took us a while to find you.'

12

'That was the idea.'

Cambridge University Press 2010
Merion Taylor's 'V' and the evolution of the post-gendered gaze.
In this provocative new study, the Professor of Cultural Practice at Sussex University argues that the response to Merion Taylor's seminal portrait 'V' represents an early articulation of emerging ideas around the female gaze and, as such, the painting has a key role to play in defining parameters for a post gendered art history practice in the future.

'How long have you been living here?'

'Since my niece did the conversion. We call it the granny attic because everyone thinks I'm her grandmother. Lovely, isn't it?'

'Very nice. And the new name?'

'Sorry, I couldn't resist it.'

Sky News 2016
A famous painting from the 1960s is back in the news for the second time this month. Merion Taylor's 'V' was infamous in its day. Looking at it now, it's hard to understand what all the fuss was about, but back in the swinging 60s (ask your grandparents, kids) this painting sent shock waves through polite society. Everybody from pop stars to the Prime Minster got involved. The Archbishop of Canterbury declared it 'A serious threat to the nation's moral health'. Well, three weeks ago that threat was finally removed. A woman entered the Tate Modern where a retrospective of Taylor's work was on show and slashed the famous canvas in three places.

And this week the plot thickened when the damaged painting was declared a fake. Experts brought in to examine the canvas said it was painted within the last decade. A red-faced spokesperson for the Tate admitted, 'We should have noticed. The brushwork clearly lacks the finesse of the original'. A police enquiry is underway.

'By the way, I recognised your niece. From the CCTV. She's the woman who slashed the painting, isn't she?'

'And do you recognise me, Inspector?'

'To be honest, no.'

'It's ok, Inspector, you're allowed to stare. Hard to believe it's the same face, isn't it? Nobody would recognise me in the street now, would they? But then Merion Taylor took the original — he stole it and gave it to 'V'.'

'And now he's given it back?'

'I have the painting, if that's what you mean. It arrived a year ago. He left instructions in his will — returning stolen goods, he called it. Bit bloody late.'

'And the copy?'

'Merion, of course. I did laugh when they said the brushwork wasn't up to much. He was in the early stages of Parkinson's when he painted it but, still, he would have been so offended.'

'So, where is it now? Where is 'V'?'

She's in the garden.'

'In the shed?'

'No, in the garden.'

Newsnight October 2017

Report by Arts Editor, Mary Sullivan.

One of the iconic images of the 60s permissive society is gone forever, we learnt today. 'V' by Merion Taylor has divided opinion for the last five decades, but whether you loved it or loathed it, you had to have been living in a cupboard not to have seen it. From t-shirts to wine bottles, 'V' has been everywhere. But from now on, those reproductions are all we'll have.

Police had been searching for the painting ever since the canvas displayed in a recent Tate Modern exhibition was revealed to be a fake. Two months ago, they finally found the original – in a garden in Oxfordshire. This week, art restorers announced that the painting was beyond repair.

Insert: Maggie Williams, restorer:

'The canvas has been exposed to the elements and unprotected for too long. It is completely disfigured and decayed. There's nothing left to restore.'

Since its unveiling in the mid-60s, Taylor's painting has generated eight books, two documentaries, a graphic novel and a contemporary dance piece, as well as numerous art works and academic papers. It even featured in an episode of The Simpsons. So, it's unlikely we've seen the last of 'V'.

And in a twist that'll surely have movie writers sharpening their pencils, the garden in which police discovered the painting, turns out to be owned by the niece of Veronica Barton-Jones, the original model for 'V'. Barton-Jones, who disappeared in the late 60s and had been presumed dead, managed to escape attention by drastically changing her appearance and living quietly in the country. She also changed her name. For the last six decades, the woman who was 'V' has been living under the name of Gray. Doreen Gray.

Obituary notice. The Times November 2017
Veronica Barton-Jones, the model for the well-known painting 'V' by the artist Merion Taylor, has died in mysterious circumstances at the home she shared with her niece in Oxfordshire.

Despite the fact that Ms Barton-Jones was infirm and unable to leave the house, her death appears to have been caused by prolonged, unprotected exposure to the elements. Funeral arrangements have been postponed while further medical examinations take place.

They will come no more, the old men with their beautiful manners by Sheena Cook

A homage to Philip Larkin

Second Prize, Scottish Arts Club Short Story Competition 2022

The December Sunday had brought the snow and made the raspberry bushes white. An hour or two, and it would be gone. I spent that hour moving the jam from the cupboard to the stone shelves of the larder, shifting the store of jam my father and I had made from the fruit of these bushes.

Our farm never made anything more than a subsistence living, but its soil yielded small new potatoes that tasted of hazelnuts, the same as when I was little. Every year I went home for the first digging, eating them with melting salted butter on a June evening after the rain.

At around the same time came the first of the raspberries. My father had planted those fruit bushes among his beehives, and tended them wearing a tweed suit, trousers held up with orange baler twine, his wool undershirt open at the neck, fixing things outside, stopping to write notes for poems with a pencil into his pocket-sized hardback notebook, until he could be alone at his roll top desk.

On the first Sunday in June, I went home, and he was sitting on the doorstep in the open doorway drinking tea — a round butter biscuit spread with treacle in his other hand, possibly waiting for me, possibly not.

But the potatoes weren't ready. That day, he dug some up and said they were still green. 'You'll have to stay a few more days,' he said. 'Sunday. We'll have them next Sunday.'

I sat at the kitchen table and he brought scrambled eggs on toast, the buttery kind only he made. He tucked a tea towel under his chin and ate a bowl of raspberries, one by one, dipping each with his teaspoon into a saucer of cream, letting the ivory liquid fall from the berry back into the bowl.

My father kept most of his thoughts and feelings to himself, economical with his words, as if they might be taxed. His sentences ended unexpectedly. I always waited for more, but more never came. I'd learned to pay attention to the unsaid, to what lay between his words.

We had a secret language though; lines from poems, sometimes abridged, sometimes a mash-up of lines from various poems.

He held the last raspberry high, letting the remaining cream fall. 'As the poet said, so much depends on this, upon a red raspberry dipped in white cream falling into the bowl.'

My father still lived in my childhood home which had also been his childhood home; a stone farmhouse beside a steading where he kept cattle and sheep and a few pigs. He grew his own cabbage and kale and potatoes and made his oatmeal brose with the pale green kale broth. He hardly watched television but sat in the evenings in front of the fire beside the lamp with a book of poetry and a teacup of whisky.

I spent the week there, walking the bumpy roads of my childhood and sitting in the kitchen rocking chair beside the old piano, letting the rhythm of the farm, where time collapsed, pass at the right speed. The postman came on his bike in the middle of each weekday morning in time for elevenses; the grocer in his van on Tuesday morning with a tin of custard and pinhead oats for my father s brose; the fish man on Wednesday with lemon sole or herring for the fridge and a piece of salmon skin tossed to the blind cat; the cleaning lady on Thursday; the butcher's van on Friday with a couple of sausages or a pork chop and a few slices of black pudding, and the baker on Friday afternoons with a lemon tart, floury baps and oatcakes for the larder.

There was only time on the farm, where the best of life was lived quietly, where nothing happened but a calm journey through the day, where change was imperceptible and precious life was everything.

I spent the evenings playing the old piano. It was exactly as I left it — the open book of Chopin preludes, the old vase on top, untouched, as if to win me back.

He had wanted me, his only daughter, to go to university, so he sold the pictures off his walls, his mother's silver out of the drawers and the cattle from the field. I was sent away to learn Latin and French while he sat on his proud combine harvester, cutting barley.

We spent my last morning making a batch of jam from the raspberry bushes outside the kitchen window. He stirred the pot on the Rayburn while the red liquid bubbled. I sterilised the jam jars. His hand shook as he ladled the jam into each jar and I wiped the sides of the jars with my mother s old dishcloth. I held the cellophane covers over the top of each jar as he stretched a rubber band over them. We lined the glass jars full of the scarlet liquid on the larder shelves, more than enough for all the coming summers' and winters' teas.

The first new potatoes from the garden were finally ready, so my father poured a scull of them covered in earth into the red plastic basin in the sink. He had been right, they needed seven more days. We stood under raindrops falling on the skylight, cleaning the potatoes, my father s head bent towards mine. His old hands were better suited to fixing broken tractor axles than cleaning small potatoes. He let each badly cleaned potato fall with a splash into the basin. The purple bruises on the backs of his hands made a ghost hand reach through my ribs and squeeze my heart.

I boiled the potatoes and brought them to the table. He dipped each potato into a ramekin of melted butter and let the butter drip off, the same as he had done with the raspberries. 'Everything,' he said, 'depends upon this.'

Later, I joined my father for his walk. The long evening waved yellow with broom and the air was thick with the coconut scent of it. The sun sank on the other side of the river and he talked about the golden light with wonder, as if seeing it for the first time, or the last.

He stopped to rebuild the fallen stones of our neighbour's dry-stone dyke. That's what people did there, they stopped to fix broken things, averting someone's pain before it happened. And there was no need for the neighbour ever to know that his dry-stone dyke had been falling. Any one of my father's neighbours would do the same for him. It gave me a secure feeling, of people moving about their days, silently watching out for each other, helping the earth go around.

He walked bent forward looking at the ground, hands clasped behind his back, carrying his losses in the muscles around his spine. 'The clock,' he said, 'only ticks one way.'

We walked through the sunshine and grass into the outshift, where the fields frayed into the trees of my far-off childhood, the swallows showing us the way. We walked through the fields along the dry-stone dykes covered with spongey moss. The peasie-wits dove into the yellow broom and white butterflies landed among the daisies and folded their wings for a rest. I walked with my father into the twilight, the wolf light, the time when the familiar became wild.

'Life is long,' he said 'but not if you like it. If you like it, it's short.'

We got to the clearing in the woods where the shepherd's hut stood, which had always seemed to me like a dappled church. I used to come here when I was little to find my father, picking my way through dark patches of spilled diesel on the ground, past broken tractors drowning in nettles, along the bumpy road to the well, then down among the trees at the bottom of the bog park.

We sat now inside the shepherd's hut that had been left to moulder. Decay had made progress since I was last there, the walls now so long fallen that moss had enveloped the stones. The red formica table I'd dragged there still sat between two tree stumps.

'The doctor told me it's bone marrow cancer,' he said, out of nowhere. 'If you're lucky to survive that, you get acute leukaemia.'

That ghost hand dug its nails into my heart. I waited for him to say more, but he didn't.

He turned to the red table and put his palms flat on it, as if he could no longer bear his own weight. He looked into my face for a long moment. I didn't know whether he was examining me for a reaction or pleading for help. I waited.

He lowered his head, taking a moment to listen to his heart and find the right words. 'It's a richt scunner,' he said, using one of his usual understatements. His sentences contained fewer words than necessary, every other word unspoken, so that I never knew if he meant one thing or another. He could have meant that becoming ill was a scunner or having hands too awkward to scrub small potatoes or ladle jam into jars was a scunner.

In the middle of the silence, before I could ask how long he had left, he walked away.

Back at home, I lit the wood stove with the last of the winter's store of wood, then arranged a bowl of sweet peas on a tray and made a pot of tea and spread my father's favourite treacle on an Orkney oatcake and we sat in the sitting room on the sofa next to each other, resting our feet on the wooden table. The logs burned in the stove, scenting the air with woodsmoke as wind gusted around us outside and rain hurled itself at the window panes. The poetry volumes packed onto the shelves above our heads would not be consulted tonight.

I sat with him while we gave each other time to work out how ill he was, and I pictured him alone in the farmhouse in front of the fire, pretending not to need help, not wanting to cause a fuss by phoning the doctor to ask for a home visit. What would happen when he could no longer drive? If he fell in the night, lying quietly in pain on the flagstone floor in his pyjamas, who would he cry out to? The hand tightened around my heart.

'We'll get a nurse in during the night,' I said, 'and I'll come up at weekends and as often as I can.'

I said it was time to stop hauling himself underneath tractors to fix them, pay for a farm manager instead, and sit in his deck chair in the garden with the sun on his face and the breeze in his hair, listening to the shipping forecast on the radio warning about gales losing their identity over the Atlantic until the end of his days. But we both knew he wouldn't. He would sit on his beloved tractor until his last day.

The next morning, before I left to go back to Edinburgh, I came out of the sitting room at the same time as he emerged from his study, and we hugged long and hard. Neither of us spoke.

As I was about to drive away, he leaned through the car window and said, 'The sweet peas, they're sweeter than all the rest.'

All along the farm road, I kept glancing into my rear-view mirror and he was still there, one hand raised in a farewell, growing smaller and smaller.

On this December Sunday, I finished moving the jars of jam, which now he would not sit and eat. He had put his last summer into those jars, sweet and meaningless, as the poet said, and not to come again.

The Witch
by David Butler

Third Prize, Scottish Arts Club Short Story Competition 2022

The Hegarty place was a half-mile out the canal, between the lock and the humpbacked bridge. It was on the far side, which only had a rough path running along it. It wasn't what you'd call a house, either. More a couple of shacks thrown together slap-dash in a yard full of nettles and burdocks and an old bathtub filled with empty bottles.

'Before planning permission was a thing,' their da said. Joseph Donlon TD had been Town Councillor before he got into the Dáil on the third count.

'An oul sympathy vote,' Blinky Roche sneered, giving Joey a sneaky dig in the back. Because it was only a year after their mother died. Blinky Roche's da had been deselected by the party for openly criticising Mr Lemass.

Siobhán once asked their da how come such a monstrosity had been allowed in the first place. After that, Joey could never think of the Hegarty place without thinking of the word monstrosity. And the bloody mongrel that was kept chained to the gate was a right monster you'd want to steer well clear of any time you were passing there on your bike. At one time, there was meant to be a whole tribe of Hegarty children running wild out there. But now it was just Bridie Hegarty, living on her own with cats and hens and a goat up on the roof. And that vicious oul tyke she kept chained to the gate. She looked like a red Indian squaw, face all wrinkled and smoky, hair a mad grey tangle.

'All her kids were taken off her by Social Services,' Siobhán said.

'And weren't they right,' said their Aunt Ciara, 'and her a dipso?' It must be sad, though, to have all of your kids taken away.

There were all sorts of stories doing the rounds about Bridie Hegarty. How she was an oul witch who sowed ragwort in fields at night to poison the cattle. How she could make an animal miscarry by giving it the evil eye. How she drowned puppies in a rough sack. How she was arrested twice for drunk and disorderly, and once for scratching the policeman's face who was arresting her. But there were other stories. How she'd been a nurse over in England during the war. Then she'd come back afterwards with an English squaddie who had skin grafts and nightmares where he shouted out. It was that squaddie who'd knocked together the shacks out on old Dinny Hegarty's scrap of land out the canal. Then within the year he'd upped and left, though Titch Brennan said that wasn't true, and that Bridie Hegarty kept him chained up inside the shack to this day. Siobhán said that no-one knew who the fathers of Bridie Hegarty's kids were, only that every one of them had had a different father. Auntie Ciara clucked and made a sour face when she said that.

Siobhán was a Mount Anville girl now. Even before the bi-election, she'd made up her mind to go to boarding-school up in Dublin. Joey could never get his head around why. He'd've sworn she was happy here, even after it was just the three of them. Or the four of them, counting Auntie Ciara who'd moved in to look after their mother when she was dying of cancer and then stayed on in the spare room. Auntie Ciara was a spinster. That was a funny word because it made Joey think of the skinny little spindle that was always spinning around on top of the Singer sewing machine she worked at every evening. But Ciara Donlon wasn't skinny. She was hefty and pious. His dad said that about her, even though she was his own flesh and blood.

Siobhán always seemed to be in flying form any weekend she came home, with her stories of high jinks in the dormitories, and eccentric nuns, and the films they got to watch every film night.

'It's a top school, Joey,' his father explained to him that first night on their own when he couldn't sleep because his gut was hollowed out and emptiness was like a fist jammed in his throat.

'Siobhán's the girl for getting ahead. You watch, and you learn, boy. With a good education behind her, there'll be no stopping her.' And sure enough, she'd come second in her class that year in the Inter cert. Though their da went spare when he saw the miniskirt and Beatle boots she wanted to go out in to celebrate.

It was a real gut-punch when Joey heard she wasn't going to be coming home for the mid-term. Siobhán always came home for Halloween. It was Siobhán who carved the pumpkin into a Jack o' Lantern and sliced up the barmbrack so each of them got something. And Siobhán organised the games their Mam used to organise — ducking for sixpences, or trying to bite coins out of a hanging apple with your hands behind your back. The thrupenny-bit was the easiest because it had so many corners. It was Siobhán who'd taken him down to the huge bonfire they always had on the green in the council estate. Every year they'd stack tyres and all sorts of rubbish for weeks beforehand, even though the guards were forever saying it was illegal.

Then a couple of weeks ago he'd overheard his da and Siobhán having a real shouting match on the phone. He was upstairs in his room and all he heard through the floorboards was his da's side. 'I will not stand by and have this family disgraced,' and 'If your poor mother was alive,' and 'Have you no thought for anyone but yourself?' And after that his da had been livid for days, barely speaking to him, Joey, though it was hardly his fault. And the upshot was, Siobhán wouldn't be coming home for Halloween this year. And to make matters worse their da would be staying over up in Dublin too. 'On Dáil business,' he said. So Joey was supposed to stay stuck in the house with Auntie Ciara for company.

So when Titch Brennan and Blinky Roche said they were planning a raid on the Hegarty place with bangers and sparklers and a couple of fireworks smuggled down from the North by Roche's da, and was he game for it, Joey said yeah. But all day it gave him a worry pain. And it wasn't because he was scared, either. It was because one day back in fourth class he was playing soldiers with

Stephen Madden down by the lock when Bridie Hegarty came along, wrapped up in that filthy coat she always wore that smelled of piss and was more a blanket with buttons than a coat. And Stephen Madden, who was a bit of a daredevil, stood out in front of her and asked her straight out, 'What was it like during the war?'

She looked shocked to hear the question. She was too used to schoolkids sniggering and mocking and firing stones at her shack from the town side of the canal. And the upshot was, she brought Steven Madden in past the dog who just sniffed at him and on into her shack and when he returned he had a wooden box the squaddie must've left behind with medals and cap-badges and bullet-cases and best of all an Iron Cross that he'd took off a dead Gerry. All that year, that box was their treasure-chest in the secret den that even Siobhán didn't know about. But then Steven Madden's family moved away.

Titch Brennan said they weren't doing no cowardly long-range attack from the town side of the canal like the St Declan's boys. They were going all the way inside the compound so they were. There was a gap in the fence round the back where the mongrel couldn't see them and even if he could the chain wouldn't reach. They'd rendezvous at the lock at twenty hundred, and go in after dark. Then they'd make their getaway down the other direction to where the humpbacked bridge was.

Joey knew well he'd get into trouble. After tea Auntie Ciara said it was ok for him to go trick or treating, but not to go anywhere near the bonfire on the council estate and to be sure to be back home by eight o'clock. He was eleven, for God's sake! Besides, eight was no damn good. They were only meeting up at eight o'clock.

If his da had of been home he'd never have dared stay out, that's for sure.

It was overcast, but it looked like the drizzle would hold off. They lay at the gap in the wire fence, all three of them, their faces darkened with mud like commandos. But first they needed a volunteer to do a recce. And since Joey hadn't brought any of the ammunition, Titch Brennan said it was down to him to go in. There was no electricity in the Hegarty place, but there must've been an oil-lamp lit because there was a buttery light glowing from the back window.

His heart hammering, Joey crawled through the gap in the fence. Twice he looked back at the four eyes that were peering after him from between the dock leaves. The sick yellow moon smouldering behind the clouds seemed to give those eyes a malevolent glimmer. There was a coal scuttle by the old bathtub. He hauled it over to the window, slowly so as not to let it clank. Then he carefully climbed onto it to have a look in.

Everything was blurred. It was as if the glass was sweating on the inside.

But there, sprawled on the kitchen table inside the window, he made out something absolutely crazy. It was shaped like a huge white letter M. But it was like the graffiti M scrawled up in the jacks that Blinky Roche had shown him and sniggered at. An M that was meant to be a pair of women's legs spread out knees up with her bits on show. And there on the kitchen table, through the blur, the feet of the M had stockings on and now he could make out the rest of the girl's body lying down flat on the table going away from him with the skirt thrown up over her tummy. And now at this end stooping between the stockinged feet, there was Bridie Hegarty's head, all bleary like it was underwater, but he knew it from the tangle of greasy hair that fell thick as brambles. But what was she doing? She had some sort of a plastic bottle or tube in her hand. And then the other person, the one flat on the table moved her head and seemed to look up straight at him and Jesus, oh Jesus Christ! Oh Jesus Christ!

The coal-scuttle teetered and his leg slipped. He crashed over upending it. At once the mongrel let out a torrent of barks and he heard the chain rattle and catch. And he was already scrambling for it.

He tumbled out over the fence and ran like crazy, ran away from the cascade of barking in the direction of the bridge this time, ran blindly, heart hammering and breath raw and eyes wobbly with tears and just when he got to the bridge he ran straight bang into his father. Which was crazy because his father was up in Dublin.

But there was the TD's Hillman Minx parked in where you couldn't see it from the road and that was his da's heavy tweed overcoat he was grabbing hold of and burying his nose into.

Joey looked up into the shocked white face and he cried, 'Da, she's got Siobhán, Da! We have to help her! She's got Siobhán inside there, Da!'. But already the gloved hand was clamped tight over his mouth and his father's voice hissed, 'Would you shut up to fuck for Christ's sake Joey.'

Evening in the Tropics
by Mike Lunan

Winner, Isobel Lodge Award 2022
Shortlisted, Scottish Arts Club Short Story Competition 2022

Every evening at sunset the dogs began to gather. They came from all directions, some singly, some in small groups, mongrels for the most part. Some came from across the canal, others along the road which ran along the front of the bomb-site. The few passers-by were accustomed to seeing them but they were so much part of the furniture, as it were, that nobody gave them any thought. By the time it was fully dark there must have been thirty or more, waiting patiently, silently. Eventually a door opened at the rear of the building and the dogs ran in eagerly.

Before the fighting there had been three buildings on that side of the road — a grand hotel well past its heyday, a smaller annex where the hotel staff had had their quarters, a large general store. The bomb had been a direct hit on the store and because it had fallen when it did, the store had been full of women with small children shopping while their menfolk were at work and the older children at school. There had been so many killed that ever since that part of the town had been avoided as being fated. The annex had been badly damaged but still stood. The hotel, which had been empty at the time, had escaped damage apart from broken windows.

Years later the hotel had been sold to a European couple who re-opened it. The guests were mainly elderly foreigners, couples, mostly Europeans but with a few Americans. Most stayed for a few nights, but something about the hotel was clearly attractive — despite its location — and many guests returned, usually staying for a week at most. Locals who passed were mildly curious about what attracted rich foreigners – for clearly they had to be rich to stay in a big hotel — to the city, indeed to the country itself, but there was no way to understand these rich foreigners.

Guests usually arrived in the afternoon when the daily flight landed in the hottest part of the day. They were met by an air-conditioned bus which brought them the 15 miles to the city. Their hosts knew that their journeys would have been uncomfortable, for the only airline serving the city after the fighting was still the old regime's carrier, its planes nearly 40 years old and never particularly welcoming even in the good times. The air-conditioned bus was the first step in making the guests more comfortable, a process continued when on arrival at the hotel they were met with cold drinks and snacks. Alcohol was of course not served — at least, not then. New arrivals might be unwelcome observers, and trust had to be earned. It would not do for the hotel to attract suspicion from the religious leaders. Registration followed and guests were conducted to their rooms to rest. Dinner would be at sunset.

Dinner on the first night was always of the highest standard. Guests were astonished to find such excellent cuisine in a run-down city, but the hotel's owners had shrewdly persuaded a French chef to join them (for a share of the profits) and, as he had some knowledge of the country from its colonial days, he was willing to do so. After dinner the guests were gathered in the lounge to hear what was planned for them. As well as the owners the doctor and the nurses were there, sitting quietly at the back of the room.

Coffee was served and introductions were made. On this occasion there were two new couples (from Berlin and Paris) and a returning couple from Miami. All were in their mid-eighties. The two European men were in wheelchairs and the American woman was blind.

The owners introduced Dr Todd, who explained what the procedure would be. At the appropriate time the treatment would be given. He said that the requirements were much less onerous that was the case in Switzerland, making it less troublesome to use his services. All that was needed was the agreement of the wife or husband, and payment of the necessary fee. He expected that some couples would wish to go away and take time to come to a decision, and he was glad to see that Mr and Mrs Hayward had returned. Were they now ready to proceed?

Lucy Hayward said she was but would prefer to wait until tomorrow so that she could feel the warmth of the sun one more time. Her treatment was arranged for noon the next day.

This led the German and French couples to announce that they had no need to go away and think, and that the two men would be happy to have their treatments tomorrow as well. Dr Todd pointed out that he couldn't carry out more than one treatment at a time, but that he would be happy to do one in the morning and two in the afternoon.

At 10 the next morning, Frau Frick wheeled her husband to the treatment room where Dr Todd and the nurses were waiting. The younger nurse prepared him for the treatment while the older nurse took Frau Frick away to the next room to sign the necessary papers and pay the fee — $50,000 in cash. The nurse then took care of all the ensuing formalities with Frau Frick. At noon a similar procedure took place for Lucy Hayward and her husband, and another for Henri and Marie Bonnard during the afternoon. None of the guests would be leaving.

That evening at sunset the dogs began to gather. They came from all directions, some singly, some in small groups, mongrels for the most part. Some came from across the canal, others along the road which ran along the front of the bomb-site. The few passers-by were accustomed to seeing them but they were so much part of the furniture, as it were, that nobody gave them any thought. By the time it was fully dark there must have been thirty or more, waiting patiently, silently. Eventually a door opened at the rear of the building and the dogs ran in eagerly. They fed well that evening.

The Letter from the Home Office
by Gail Anderson

Winner, Edinburgh Award for Flash Fiction 2022

It spins up on a thermal, fluttering in a sparrow-brown envelope (second class) and when she reaches to catch it, her hot-air balloon lurches. Eleven years aloft in a brittle basket of willow, a moth-wing billow overhead. A hailstorm might send her plummeting, a hurricane spiralling stratospheric. She longs to land — but she is not allowed. When gravity pulls, she feeds the hungry burner forms and proofs, fistfuls of cash, until the firebox burns bright. It's hard work, staying up — but the view is striking. Green quilts hemmed in hawthorn, ruched with oak and ash. A molecule of sheepdog moves a puddle of milk between meadows. She counts hours on a clock of standing stones. From this height history's hard edges are buried. Children wave as she floats overhead. Adults squint up, shielding their eyes. 'Are you on holiday?' 'When do you go home?' Their tinny voices fizz her ether. There are days she wishes for the storm that would blow her far away from this place. But now, sliding her thumb under the brown paper flap, reading the words inside, the seams of her rainbow silk start to shred. Down she goes: through clouds, past radio towers, pigeons dodging. Past bored office-block faces, tumbling through horn-blasting, flag-waving air, the street rushing to meet her in a stink of bins and wet and diesel. Belonging here, she knows, will be a new kind of distance. This is the price of the ground beneath her feet.

Sea Fret
by Kathy Hoyle

Second Prize, Edinburgh Award for Flash Fiction 2022

Sea listens.

Boys. Three boys. Lithe-limbed boys with windswept curls, slipping on seaweed, clinging and climbing on mossy rocks, catcalling through cupped hands. Boys, who bellow dares and whoop and push and land in icy sea foam spray, voices on the cusp of breaking.

Sea wants.

Boys. Three boys. Bare-chested boys with mammal blood and thumping hearts and slick white bone, not salted shell or rough-scaled fin. Boys, who taste of youth and joy and fragrant grass on summer days. Boys who bravely dive from rusted pier to swelling tide, ignoring warning voices echoing on crested waves.

Sea takes.

Boy. Smallest boy. Sweet plump boy with fading breath and aching legs and fingertips that briefly touch then slip away. Boy, whose mother — just that morning — packed him rounds of buttered bread and apple cake and warned of vicious sea with riptide curl and unseen snarling teeth below. Smallest boy, with tiny final cry, drowned out by sound of beating mammal hearts and screams from voices on the cusp of breaking.

Sea leaves.

Boys. Two boys. Lithe-limbed boys with bare chests heaving, salted tears on milk-pale cheeks, standing deathly still on sharp-stoned shore. Boys who start to shiver, clammy cold together, as they watch the sea fret mist roll in to haunt their minds with guilt-soaked dreams, forever.

Things visible and invisible
by Michael Callaghan

Third Prize, Edinburgh Award for Flash Fiction 2022

I am disturbed by the sound of crying.

Annie, I think.

I look at my sleeping wife, sigh, and make my way towards Annie's bedroom. Looking in, I see the mounded bedclothes.

I go over, pull back the covers.

Annie's eyes open wide. Then she smiles.

'Daddy...' she says.

I kiss her head. She smells of soap and strawberries.

'Bad dream?'

Annie nods. 'A *monster* chased me.'

'Monsters? Honestly!' I smile, then check her closet and behind her cabinet. Finally, I look under her bed. And here I look worried.

'Wait... what's... this...?'

I reach under the bed, then bring my hand back... in a claw shape.

'The *Tickle* Monster!' I say. And I tickle her until she squeals with laughter.

Then she stops, and looks serious.

'Tonight's Halloween, Daddy.' she says. 'Halloween brings out *ghosts*.'

I smile. 'Halloween doesn't bring *out* ghosts. They're always there. But they're harmless. At Halloween the boundaries between the living world and the spirit world just get more... see-through.'

'But... I worry about... dying, Daddy.'

'You won't die, Annie.'

'But I *could!* That car accident. I was nearly *killed...*'

'But you weren't. You were okay.' I stroke her head. Annie looks at me.

'But... you weren't okay, Daddy.'

I glance at the window. It's getting light.

'No... I wasn't. But... I'm always with you, Annie. Remember that. Remember...'

Annie turns away.

'It's nearly morning, Daddy.'

Then she shimmers and distorts, her image fading and shrinking until she vanishes completely, and I am alone again in the darkness.

Taenia Saginata's Last Words
by Andrew Gardiner

Winner of the Golden Hare Award 2022
Shortlisted, Edinburgh Award for Flash Fiction 2022

Just ca' me Tina if it's ony easier. We're a' genders thegither here. Ma pronoun's 'they' so it is.

Ma life's been absorbin' but noo ma number's up. I always aimed tae avoid harmin' yous. Hurtin' folk (or the coos, placid beasts, that yous eat) is no' whit am aboot. We ken this well enough, us tape wurms, it's in oor genes. We never *intend* tae harm, that's the difference wi' us. But now am hurt so a' am. Mortal hurt.

Lookin' back, ma life's been in sections: the grass section, coo section, and noo the in-yer-gut section. Things go roun an' roun. I was a chip aff the auld block, we a' were, a' 2000 o' us wee nippers. Pros frae the start, we already knew whit tae dae in life — nae choice, y'see. There was a youthfu' spell o' independent dauners seekin' greener pasture, but the final destination was aye the same. We're predestined, nae escape. It was jist a question o' gettin' stuck in tae yer work, inside a' the while.

The food processin' business! But it wasnae all tak, tak, tak. It's mair subtle than that, cosy even. We coorie doon inside yer guts an' gie sumthin back — fine tunin' yer immune cells, increasin' yer tolerances. We grow attached tae ye, ken?

Noo it's a' unravellin'. Am finished. Am poisoned. Am losing ma grip on ye, and ye're ma whole life so ye are. Without ye, am a goner. Will ye mourn me?

Three Fish Suppers
by Lyn Irving

Shortlisted, Scottish Arts Club Short Story Competition 2022

I stood behind the bar of McIntosh's pub and watched the door. I'd been open since five o'clock and still not served a customer. No surprise really as I listened to the harsh November rain rattle against the old windows. Suddenly the door burst open and a man blew in. Caught up in the storm, soaking wet, his head pulled down deep inside his collar he growled, 'A large whisky and a half pint.'

His voice sounded familiar and I watched nervously as he came towards the bar.

'Is there a problem? Can you no move? I asked for a drink.'

I set the whisky down and watched it trembling in the glass.

He downed it in one. His mean lips pursing tightly as he pushed the empty towards me and said, 'Put another whisky in there and where's that beer?'

With sweat slowly trickling down my neck and under the collar of my new blouse I said, 'That'll be four shillings, please.'

He looked up sharply piercing me with black, beady eyes and said 'Don't sound so worried. I can pay — look,' and he peeled a fiver from a bundle of cash and threw it on the bar. 'It's ok — relax for fucks sake — just put this bag in the box over there and then we can both take it easy,' and handing me a canvas bag he nodded towards a cardboard box that was sitting in the cubby hole McIntosh liked to call his office.

The bag clunked against the counter as I lifted it and said, 'It's heavy — what's in it?'

'What's in it? You must be new here or you'd know better than to ask such bloody stupid questions. McIntosh likes his customers to put some things out of sight – just in case of a wee bit bother later on — know what I mean?'

I didn't, but I knew he was trouble.

'Give me ten woodbine and a box of matches — no make it twenty Capstan Full Strength— and pass me a towel.'

I handed him a dishtowel, watching him take off his cheap raincoat, his bony shoulders soaked through and still hunched against the cold.

Like a shiny cormorant surfacing the water, he shook his long, black, greasy head out of the towel and said 'I'm sure I know you — have you always been a blonde?'

I thought it best to stay quiet. Instead, I gave him my best barmaid smile and pushed my breasts up front. I'd worked in pubs long enough to know how to change the subject.

'Smoke?' he said holding out the packet.

'No thanks.' I didn't want anything he had to offer.

He lit up and taking a deep draw he looked me up and down. 'Not bad – not bad at all. It's about time McIntosh had a good-looking barmaid in here. 'Good legs,' he continued as he leered over the bar, 'I like the mini skirt — suits you — what's your name?'

'Jean — it's my first night here and you're my first customer.'

'Right, well Jean, this is your lucky night, let me buy you a drink. I'm Billy, what's your poison?' and through thin lips and bad teeth he gave me a nicotine grin.

Poison or not I needed a drink, 'I'll have a whisky and lemonade.'

I backed off and poured myself a drink — my heart thumping loudly through the room. The whisky felt good. It steadied me as I held his gaze and, before either of us could speak, the door swung open and a gang of workmen poured in.

Within half an hour the place was full of hard drinking men, glad of the company and the cheer that a few payday drinks would buy. Through the fog of cigarette smoke an orange glow radiated from the wall lights and warmed the dark wooden furniture and fake leather seating. I kept busy as the men would probably spend much of their wages tonight — but that wasn't my concern as I began to enjoy their laughter and jokes.

Around nine o'clock two uniformed policemen walked in. The bar fell silent. 'Is McIntosh in? We'd like word,' said the sergeant.

'No, but I'm expecting him soon,' I replied.

'Aye well, maybe you can help. Earlier tonight, around six, there was a shooting up Maryhill Road — near the canal. We've a witness says he saw a man running down here just after it happened. Did any of these men come in around then?' The men stayed silent looking down into their drinks. The slow tick of the clock sounded high above me on the gantry, like in an old Western the first person to move would die. My eyes turned towards Billy who sat with his back against the wall, head down like the rest of the men. I thought of my two girls home alone and looked down into my whisky.

The sergeant pulled his shoulders back and stood tall as he menaced into the middle of the room: 'Come on now! Someone here must know something — it's not the first time this guy's shot somebody. You'll all be safer when he's off the streets.'

I knew he was right but heads stayed down and no-one met his eye.

Just then, the door of the snug swung open and the voice of my new boss Mcintosh boomed, 'Come on Charlie you know all these men come in here at the same time on a Friday night, at shift change from the depot! Jean doesn't know the lads in here, it's her first night. Come on through to the snug lads, maybe I can help – at least let me give you a wee dram, I'm in need of one myself — it's a wild night. Jean, pour three large whiskies and bring them on through.'

I did as I was told and soon followed Davie and the police into the snug, setting down the drinks, and leaving before they had time to ask any more questions. On my way back I stopped off at the cubby hole — a freshen up of my lipstick and a quick comb through of my hair helped steady me. Beneath the mirror sat the box where

I'd stashed Billy's bag. I didn't need to look to know there was a gun in there, I'd guessed as soon as he handed me the bag. The unmistakeable acrid smell of a recently fired weapon was something I understood only too well. My dad had brought a gun home from the war — that was his story — saying it would help keep us safe from some of the low life that lived in our tenement slums. Well, it hadn't kept him safe, but who knows, maybe this time he'd be right.

I went out to serve last orders just in time to see Billy's shiny black coat duck out the front door. The pub emptied quickly and within fifteen minutes of closing time I'd cleared the tables and washed the empties. Then into the cubby hole to put on a bit more lipstick before putting on my hat, coat and gloves. I watched in the mirror as the pull of the gun turned my head towards the cardboard box. 'Yes, gloves would be important,' I thought as I lifted it out and turned it over in my hands, getting a feel for it — feeling it's comforting weight — its confidence — its power. It dropped into my bag. 'That's me off now Mr McIntosh,' I said, popping my head round the snug door.

'Right you are Jean, see you tomorrow. Just put out the bar lights and pull the door closed behind you.'

The weather was still bloody wild, freezing rain driving sharp into my face. I hurried on, the sound of my stiletto heels clicking loudly through the dark Glasgow tenements. I held close to their grim bulk in the hope of some shelter. I took off my shoes. They were cheap rubbish and no good in this rain. Without them it was easier to run silently through the dark, but all too soon I spotted the red glow of a cigarette in a nearby close and knew it was too late for running.

He slunk in beside me, slipping his arm round my waist, saying, 'Jean — fancy bumping into you here — why don't I walk you home? Make sure you're safe.'

'No, no, no thanks Billy. I'm fine — really — thanks.'

'Aye, but you're shivering and your feet are soaking wet. Put your shoes back on. I like the sound of a woman in high heels.'

He held me as I put on my shoes, pulling me close and putting his loose whisky lips on mine. Shuddering at the wet sour smell of him, I drew back and said, 'I live up by the canal. Are you sure you want to go up there with all those polis about?'

'For fucks sake Jean — are you mental? Those bastards are no interested unless it's one of their own — now come on. I'm soaked through — get a move on!'

The rain never let up, lashing down as he half dragged me up onto the muddy towpath. Deep puddles glittered orange from the dim street lights. My hands cracked and stiffened with the cold and my ever-tightening grip on my bag. So, as we approached a big tree creaking loudly in the wind, I licked my dry lips and spoke close in his ear, 'Give me a minute Billy, just let me go behind this tree a minute. I need to pee.' And before he could answer, I shot off through the bushes, brambles clawing at my legs. I just needed a moment to hold the gun — to steady myself — cos if there was one thing my dad taught me about guns was 'Don't rush them — take it easy — but be sure you're ready to fire — you might not get a second chance.'

'Well, yes Dad, you were right, Billy never gave you a second chance,' I thought as I looked down at the bluish sheen of the metal glinting in the rain. It felt good as it led me out from behind the tree. Billy stared at it and then at me as if in recognition but it was too late for words. The gun kicked back and the air around us exploded, my ears ringing as I watched Billy stagger towards the edge of the canal. He dropped — one arm in the water and lay motionless on the path. I edged towards him ready to fire again if he moved but he lay still as the rain battered down on his beady eyes and bloody chest. Fumbling in his coat pocket I found the bundle of cash he had flashed earlier and stuck it in my bag along with the gun. He made a bit of a splash as he rolled into the water but no-one would hear anything up here.

Pulling off my shoes again I fled silently down the path. The welcoming light of Luigi's drew me in. 'Three fish suppers, three buttered rolls and a bottle of Irn Bru please Luigi,' I gasped, suddenly able to breathe again.

'Oh, hello Jean — You ok? You look scared'

'Aye, Aye, I'm fine. It's this bloody weather — broke the heel off my shoe and had to run through the mud in my bare feet.'

'Splashing out a bit, aren't you? You usually have only one fish and three portions of chips. Is it a special occasion?'

'Aye, well you could say that Luigi. Started my new job tonight — barmaid — down Mcintosh's pub — thought I would treat the girls now I've got some money.'

A Lesson on Conditionals
by Kirsty Hammond

Commendation, Edinburgh Award for Flash Fiction 2022

Okay class, quiet down. Does anyone know what a conditional is? No?

A conditional is a sentence, usually starting with 'if,' where one half expresses something which depends on the other half.

There are four, numbered zero to three.

The zero conditional is for situations that are always true. For example, *if a woman loses her husband, she becomes a widow.* True, even if you're only 37. Both parts of the sentence use the present tense.

The first conditional is usually true. *If you tell someone to go fuck themselves and they die, you'll hate yourself so much you'll want to smash every mirror in your house.* It's not as certain as the zero, but still likely. The structure is present tense, future tense.

The second conditional is unlikely. *If you were still here, I'd never let you go.* This isn't going to happen, no matter how hard you wish it. Past tense for the first part, *would* plus infinitive for the second.

Finally, the third conditional. Impossible situations. Past perfect, followed by *would have* plus past participle.

If I hadn't screamed at you, you wouldn't have stormed out, wouldn't have got drunk, wouldn't have tried to drive home.

If I'd known the agony I'd feel at losing you, I would've begged you to stay, hidden your car keys, told you I loved you.

What? No, I'm fine.

Anyway, your homework is to write three examples of each conditional. If you forget anything, just Google it.

See you next week.

Vibrating at the Speed of Light
by David Martin

Shortlisted, Scottish Arts Club Short Story Competition 2022

I am dying and this is my last breath. I hold on to it forever.

*

Here I am, standing in a room with men I don't know. There's a small window above my head but it doesn't let in much light and I struggle to see their faces clearly. They are rough. Jostling as they clamber about me. The vest is too big, so they add tape to plaster it tightly to my body. I stay silent, not wanting to show any weakness. I feel special. They chose me because I am strong.

They turn to another man in the corner. I hadn't noticed him at first but now the room empties and there's just him and me. He comes closer and bends down. His beard is only a few inches from my face and I smell the tobacco on his breath.

'Paradise awaits you', he whispers. I bow my head, not knowing if I should answer.

The vest is padded with rusty screws and bolts that dig into my chest. He is carefully packing explosives into specially made pockets, adjusting them so the wires sit neatly. Checking, one at a time, before moving on to the next. My heart races but still I remain, silent.

He twists the wires together and gives them a tug to ensure everything is as it should be, then feeds them through my sleeve so the free ends hang below my wrist. He fastens my shirt and winds a black tie around my collar before tying a respectable knot.

He looks approvingly at his work. It's hard to move. My body feels stiff. He helps me into a waistcoat designed to hide the bulky vest. And now my jacket. He is praying for me. I can see in his eyes that he fully believes in what we are doing. I wish I had such unfaltering faith. 'Your father would be proud if he could see you now', he smiles. It's meant to put me at ease.

I stare straight ahead, unflinching. I will die for a cause that is greater than me. I was nothing in this world but now I have a purpose. I will be celebrated as a martyr and my name will live on forever. My mother will want for nothing, they will make sure of that. The photographs he takes of me now will adorn the walls around our house, a daily reminder of all I have done.

*

Sitting on a metal bench in the back of the truck, I feel a shudder jolt up my spine as we hit a hole in the road. A remnant from a blast several months before. Twisting this way and that, we avoid more of these perilous obstacles. Perhaps secretly, I pray for the bomb to detonate now and spare me the horrors to come. An accident without dishonour but I know I must be strong for just a little longer. God will reward me for destroying our enemies and forgive all my sins.

I look out of the window and marvel at the foreboding Koh-i-Baba mountains. The snow drips down like white treacle from their peaks. It's as though I am seeing them for the first time and maybe I am. I cannot recollect truly looking before. The lush fields of the valley ahead welcome us, not knowing what we bring.

There are two men with me. The driver's elbow juts out of the window and every so often he sucks hard on the cigarette held between his tar-stained fingers. He could be my father if he were still alive. And now I think of my father. It troubles me that at this of all moments, I cannot remember his face. The other is about sixteen, a year older than me. His hair is tied back and he grips the side of the truck tightly. He has a knife with a bone handle tucked into a scabbard on his belt and he tracks every movement I make with his dark brown eyes.

The road is dry. Chalky dust bellows from a truck in front, weighed down with hessian sacks full of rice. A man on a motorcycle swerves to avoid a cow that has strayed onto the track as the young boy sitting behind him holds on, ever more tightly. I will do this for him. For all our people.

44

I was an outsider. My mother sent me to school in Helmand Province but my madrassa teachers saw something in me. They moved me to a madrassa in Pakistan so I could improve my studies. I was part of a family there; we all had a common purpose. I haven't seen my mother since I left but now, I am back. They have saved me from hell and for that I rejoice. How I wish she was here to see how strong I've become.

The air is colder as we approach our destination. My teacher brought me here a week ago to prepare and we sat for an hour, watching from a safe distance. We come to a halt opposite the main hall. The younger man steps out to check we are unseen. Now the driver gets into the back with me. He attaches a detonator to the loose wires. This is not his first time and it takes only a few short seconds. He looks me up and down. I know what I must do. I grip the trigger tightly and he arms the explosives.

*

I am standing at the door to the hall. Everyone is inside and these are my last moments on this world. I check my grip on the trigger remains strong. The women are on the other side of the door. The men's entrance is around the corner. I look back as my two companions watch on. I stand tall and push the door open.

I've never been to a wedding. The room is packed. Some women are dancing to music whilst others sit around tables, chatting. They are adorned with gold jewellery. Their faces painted brightly. In the corner is a large television showing the men on the other side of the partition similarly enjoying the festivities. I hear their voices clearly through the divide. In the centre of the hall is a young woman, dressed in a flowing, white dress and green shawl. Others surround her. I know at once she is the bride.

My breathing is slow and my head is clear. I am at peace with what I'm about to do. My whole life has led to this moment and I will not fail. A girl catches my gaze. Her pale green eyes are mesmerizing. I grip the trigger ever more tightly, then let go.

I wait for the end but nothing happens. The detonator has failed. The girl reaches over and grabs my arm. Pulling a shawl over her head, she leads me outside.

'You mustn't be in here,' she says sternly, 'It's forbidden.' I follow without resistance. She points to the men's entrance. 'That's for you.'

I stare at the truck as the younger man gets out, only to be called back swiftly by his elder. Tears stream down my face and I pause to wipe them away.

She is surprised by my reaction and no longer angry. 'Don't worry. It was a simple mistake. The doors should be labelled more clearly.' This girl knows nothing of what I have done. Of what I was about to do.

'I can't...' I utter, edging backwards whilst facing the truck. Immediately terrified of the younger man as he rests a hand on his knife. No more than a dozen paces from where we are standing, his rage is clear.

For a moment she looks on, confused. 'It's alright,' she shouts across to him,

'He entered the women's side by mistake.' The younger man remains poised.

'Forgive me...' I sob, yet the words are lost. No longer restrained by the older man in the cab of the truck, he begins to move towards us. Sensing danger, the girl looks one way, then the other but everyone else is inside.

'Come with me.' She leads me down a path beside the hall, empty apart from crates of Fanta and Coca-Cola. We round a corner. Now another. Running swiftly. The whole town is at the wedding and our path is clear except for an old woman who tuts loudly as we pass by. The girl tightens her head scarf and continues on, undeterred.

Suddenly unsure, I consider turning back. I could still explain what happened, it wasn't my fault, they would understand. Perhaps it wasn't too late and we could try again. Yet before those thoughts have truly taken shape, they vanish once more. And now I follow, unquestioningly. Deeper and deeper into the unknown.

The hidden paths quickly take us far away from everyone and everything and we come to a small hut with old, mismatched wooden boards for walls and a corrugated metal roof. The girl beckons me inside. 'Wait here,' she utters. 'I'll return in a few minutes.'

As soon as she leaves, I slip off my jacket, now my waistcoat. My shirt is wet with sweat and sticks to me. I struggle to pull it from my body, ashamed of what lies beneath. I feel panic at the thought of her catching me like this. Of learning the truth. There is a scythe hanging on the wall and I grab it. I cut the tape securing the vest, before tearing it from my torso. My skin bears the indents of my deadly load. I hide the vest and all its shame under some rags in the corner, and pull on my shirt once more.

The door opens and I follow her outside where there are two horses waiting. She jumps onto a magnificent black stallion with such ease that I am immediately taken aback by her confidence. I put my foot on the stirrup of the smaller, white mare. It's been a long time but I remember quickly. Now we are riding. Minutes or hours pass in an instant. We are far away from the village and its people. I follow this slight Shi`a girl, without fear. Faster and faster, the horses gallop rhythmically, one behind the other. Their breathing entrances me. I am transported to another life.

We slow to a canter and now we are laughing. The sun beats down on us and there is nobody around for miles. It feels like we are the last people alive on this world and I long for that to be true.

The barley fields are behind us, replaced by deep, blood-red poppies in full bloom. In all directions, far into the distance. The flowers swaying in the gentle breeze. Echoing the effects of the powerful narcotics they produce; my eyes feel heavy. I remember home. My mother is standing waiting for me, my father by her side. Long before the struggles we endured, when there was nothing of these things in our world. Perhaps this is someone else's memory. I

47

can't be sure. Like the paintings on the wall of the Pakistani madrassa. Paradise. In the distance, rivers of milk and honey. We dismount and walk hand in hand. The eternal afterlife. My reward.

I feel the vibrations. We are standing side by side. My chest tightens. There's a hole where my heart should be. The music is getting louder, people are laughing and dancing. Screaming. Her pale green eyes are mesmerizing. Is this our wedding? There is no pain, just regret. I am dying and this is my last breath. I hold on to it forever.

*

On a sunny day, in late spring, a 15-year-old boy, recruited as a suicide bomber by the Islamic state, enters a hall in a small Hazara town near the central highlands of Afghanistan. There are multiple casualties from the resultant blast, among them a 14year-old Shi`a girl celebrating her sister's wedding.

How to Draw a Frog
by Bruce Meyer

Editor's Prize, Edinburgh Award for Flash Fiction 2022

Successful artists ensure the frog is not dead. A live frog adds a degree of verity to the drawing process. The artist must be quick to capture the impulsive movements of the subject. Frogs are easily distracted. Inert, docile amphibians are best but hard to find.

Avoid dead frogs. They lack something, not just their lives. That goes without saying. They lose that glint in their eyes. They're easier to work with but are specimens rather than subjects. The virescent depth of their green fades. If a frog is too dead the drawing is no longer of a frog but of something returning to the mulch at the bottom of the pond. Such frogs aren't satisfactory subjects.

Some artists find success by capturing frogs in their habitat but if the creatures — frog and artists — are handled too aggressively terror ensues. Everything has a level of delicacy both artist and subject must respect. The best frogs appear happy with their circumstances. Happiness is difficult to detect but the longer a frog is studied the more its happiness becomes apparent.

Keeping a frog happy is hard work. A good artist must put a smile on the face of a little, green, Mona Lisa. Keeping company with other frogs is not enough. The best practice is to raise a frog from tadpole to a complete frog so frog and artist can trust each other in a lasting bond where a happy artist draws, and a skilled frog poses.

The Art of Convenience
by Ann Seed

Shortlisted, Scottish Arts Club Short Story Competition 2022

Howie sniffed the air. Not a whisper of wind to distill the dismal hope of nothing. Just the sea gurgling like water down the pan. He bundled up his blanket, sticky with damp autumn leaves, and trudged along the track to the gents' toilets. Every morning, before they opened to visitors, Bert let him in for tea and a shit.

Bert unlocked the turnstile and Howie shuffled through, following his benefactor into the attendant's office. The smell of disinfectant flared his nostrils.

'Have a donut,' Bert said, pouring steaming mugs of tea.

Howie shivered. The tea was like nectar and the sweetness of the donut sunlight on his tongue.

'Rough night?' asked Bert.

'Y'know. See... ma blanket's wet.'

Bert threw the mouldy blanket over a chair in front of a small electric heater then filled the sink in the corner with hot water and generous dollops of liquid soap.

'There... have a wash while I mop the floors.'

Howie scooped up the lather and pushed it into his beard, his eyes closing as an angel danced at the warmth. He wiggled off his boots and put them by the fire. What was left of his socks stuck to his stinking feet.

'Jesus, Howie!' Bert hollered, emptying his bucket and refilling it with fresh water. 'Use this, for Christ sake!'

Howie plunged in his feet. My God it felt good. Bert shut the door to keep the stench in and limped over to the mural by the turnstile. It was his labour of love, made from pebbles and shells he'd gathered from the shore. The sun shone on a rocky beach, dolphins were leaping and yachts raced full sail on a rolling sea. He ran his fingers gently over the waves...

He needed to salvage his pride and the *Coveted Convenience Competition* was the answer. Visitors had written excellent reviews, such as 'Bert's spotless domain' and 'Shipshape service!' Perhaps this was why, despite budget cuts, the Council had voted not only to keep the toilets open but to enter them in the national competition to find *Not a Convenience, but a Landmark!* By the time the judges arrived he would have the mural sparkling with a fresh coat of varnish. That might just be his ticket to redemption...

Howie headed for the exit, happily humming Roger Miller's *King of the Road.* Bert smiled. He knew Howie was familiar with every food bank and soup kitchen, and every place 'that ain't locked when no-one's around.'

Bert nipped home during a lull after lunch and, when Howie returned in the evening, he presented him with several pairs of socks. 'I've got trousers and shirts too. And scissors. Trim your beard, for Christ sake.'

'You're a goo' man, Ber',' grinned Howie, eyeing his bounty.

After their ritual cuppa, a smarter looking Howie set off for his den. It was hidden in a dense thicket of Sea Buckthorn growing untamed on the sandy hillocks beyond the shore. The spiny bushes were an efficient, if at times painful barrier against random discovery.

Howie had built his hovel from driftwood, flotsam and the rubbish people left behind on the beach. He couldn't help adding artistic flourishes. Mangled sunglasses, broken windbreaks, plastic buckets... he was never short of material. But his creative efforts were also reminders of his failed ambitions. Art was in his blood. He had tried to sculpt a living from his passion, but the results had been bankruptcy and depression. The humiliation still stung like the thorns that protected him. He hated his situation. Hated that he could seldom get enough drink to obliterate the agony.

Bert too was agonising. Although cold to his touch, his wife was always dressed to the nines. He knew what she was doing. It had been happening for months. She had disappeared again that evening. His dinner was stewing in the oven but he wasn't hungry. He sought instead the sanctuary of his study, full of the photographs he loved to take of the changing moods of the sea. But, for once, his hobby held no interest.

After a sleepless night, the scars on his disfigured leg ached. His wife had not come home. The bloody bitch had left him. He started to shave and, as he looked in the mirror, the hollow-eyed face reminded him of a vanished friend, someone he had known well and laughed with. Great, belly-busting laughs...

Waves lapped laconically and the chill air was heavy with the smell of sea salt when Howie appeared at the turnstile.

'Sorry, mate... not today,' Bert snapped.

Howie frowned. What about his shit? His tea? He shambled back to his thorny otherworld, stymied by this prickly new Bert.

Bert grabbed the bottle of whisky he kept hidden among the towels and poured a large glass. Who the hell was this loser he was helping? When Howie got hold of alcohol he became a pathetic, gibbering wreck, like the idiot who had ruined his life. Why was he bothering? Was he just being a gullible fool? And his farcical marriage... was he a fool there too? He had tried to please, to rise to the challenge of his wife's reliable misery. He had sacrificed his pride, begged her to see the worth of his hard work, to recognise that any job done well could have merit. But she had sneered and turned on her high heels.

Bert knew she had only married him to be a Navy wife. When he achieved the rank of Chief Petty Officer she had preened with the status. And oh, how she must have purred when he was away at sea. But he had worn the uniform with pride... seen some action... relished the discipline, the camaraderie... the coming home. He had loved her and it had been fun, he could kid himself, before the literal crushing blow... when his leg had been smashed to bits and life changed forever.

He remembered the shock of it... the sickening thud... the screech of brakes... the medics strapping the dripping flesh... the driver slurring his innocence... 'didn' see 'im, must've jump out d'libbrity.' And then the pain... the forced retirement... the hobbled limp...

A darkness had fallen, smothering his ambitions, shredding the last pretence of his wife's affections. He had taken solace in a simple job, an absorbing hobby, desperate to take pride in something, anything. But his wife never let him forget her disgust at their demoted status. He had tried... fought... failed...

But ex-CPO Albert S. Carstairs was a man of honour and resolve. Next morning, he arrived early at the toilets... only to find the lock had been forced, the mural shattered. Even the whisky bottle was gone. Soon after, Howie turned up looking wary after his recent rebuke. Feeling as broken as his beloved mural, Bert beckoned him in. They sat down to drink their tea.

'Sorry for yesterday, Howie. Life and that, you know? The wife's gone. Now, no mural, no landmark... and no chance in the competition.'

'Ber',' said Howie, 'You been goo' to me. A real pal.' He paused, fidgeting. 'A landmark, eh?' he continued nervously, 'Don' worry, Ber'. I migh' have an idea.'

Bert was only half listening. But, as Howie talked, he took more notice, alive to possibilities.

*

A 'Closed — Sorry for the Inconvenience' sign was pinned by the turnstile. Howie dismantled his den and passed all his best pieces to Bert who carried them to the toilets. While Bert tearfully cleared up inside, Howie, outside on the grass, began to construct two inter-locking objects from the broken mural and his piles of flotsam and junk. Slowly they began to take shape. Too slowly for Bert's liking. He wasn't even sure the plan would work.

Howie smiled at Bert's rising panic. He worked methodically day and night, energising himself with Sea Buckthorn

53

berries and tea until, finally, his 'Dancing Dolphins' artwork was complete. Bert was astonished at how lifelike the quirky creatures were. Inspired, and with hopes rising, he photographed the dolphins against his favourite view of the sea and dashed to the specialist print shop.

Later that afternoon, Bert and Howie together pasted the huge, laminated photograph over the area of the vandalised mural. The dolphins seemed to leap out over them. It was perfect.

Bert turned to Howie. 'Thanks, mate. You've saved the day! Fancy a cuppa?'

Next morning, Bert was spit-and-polishing with renewed but precarious confidence when, without notice, two besuited competition judges arrived. They inspected every inch of the gleaming premises — flushing toilets, swishing surfaces, taking notes. The whimsical dolphin statue and impressive photograph elicited nods and much whispering. The judges lingered, firing volleys of questions before leaving at last. Exhausted, Bert retreated to the office. He screwed his eyes shut tight and his silhouette dissolved in the dark...

Daily routines resumed. Echoing tiles. Disinfectant and mopping. Trying to stay sane. Supporting Howie. 'He's lost and lonely, like me,' Bert had concluded.

And then, one afternoon, a delegation descended, led by the Mayor carrying a silver cup and framed certificate.

'I am delighted to announce,' he declared, 'that our gents' toilets have won the 'Coveted Convenience Competition' for the best public conveniences in the country. Well done, Bert!'

'Your photograph! Wow!' the Mayor beamed. 'But the 'Dancing Dolphins' statue... well, that clinched it! A landmark indeed!'

When the certificate had been hung on the wall, the commotion had died down and sunset was spreading copper waves across the sky, Bert rushed home. The house was still empty. But his beautiful trophy gleamed like a beacon as he centred it on the mantelpiece. 'Public Convenience Custodian of the Year'! He chuckled softly, shaking his head.

He rubbed his chin. What now? Maybe he would look for Howie, help him rebuild his shelter. Take a bottle, get drunk. He hesitated. Who was he now? Who did he want to be? He had earned his Navy rank... it was not for nothing. Hard work, self-discipline. Even now he always wore an ironed shirt, pressed trousers. And, despite the pain in his leg, he had never missed a day's work. He could still take pride. His shoulders might be bonier but they were strong. As sure as eggs is eggs, he would make the uniform fit again.

Perhaps the old friend in the mirror hadn't vanished after all. Maybe he had just been waiting, for another mission, the call to action. Good riddance to his wife. She didn't need him. But Howie did.

Bright and breezy as the autumn sea, Bert whistled as he put the kettle on next morning. He couldn't wait for Howie to show up. It was the day he was going to flush life's shit right round the bend.

'And me and Howie,' he said out loud, 'We ain't going with it!'

Howie eventually appeared, shaking with excitement.

'They foun' me, Ber'!' he cried. 'Callin' me Flotsam, the Beach Banksy. Me, Ber'...

me!'

'The Mayor wants more sta'ues. For money!'

'Bloody brilliant!' said Bert. 'But, Howie... er, Flotsam... truth is, you're now homeless because of me. I've a spare bedroom. And I could use some help... my leg 'n all. We could give the toilets a makeover too. Your art, my photographs. What d'you say?'

'Well,' Howie replied, 'Your conveniences are cer'ainly worth coveting.'

Bert was buzzing. 'My middle name,' he said, 'Is Samuel. We could be FlotSam and JetSam, the Piss Artists!' And he started to laugh... great, belly-busting laughs...

Howie grinned, sly and satisfied. Bert's whisky and stupid mural had been easy pickings. He had the sucker's clothes... now his house... perhaps soon his job...

The pair walked home together that evening, effusive about their good fortune.

'We're flush with success!' Bert chortled, key in hand.

Bert's wife opened the door. Bert froze.

'Who the Hell's this?' she hissed, looking Howie up and down.

Howie held her gaze... winked... smiled a slow smile...

'Well,' she purred, 'I suppose you'd better come in.'

Silence
by Frances Sloan

Longlisted, Edinburgh Award for Flash Fiction 2022

'It was like a dripping tap,' Mark said. 'Just a quiet drip, drip in the background, until that day you notice it. Then it becomes a noise which grows louder in your brain. One day, you call a plumber.'

Mark left a silent order of monks just three months after entering the monastery.

He had loved the first few weeks of religious life, relishing the time to pray, to work, to escape the stream of meaningless chatter in secular life. Monastic life also made him more aware of the habits of his fellow monks.

The community ate meals in silence around the refectory table. Mark noticed a background chorus of slurps, burps, coughs, and sniffs; the volume seemed to increase daily. Brother Tim cleared his throat every five seconds. Mark had timed him.

I assumed the involuntary mealtime noises had pushed Mark to his 'call the plumber moment', but it was the actions of one monk.

Brother John had a particular breakfast routine. He always sat on Mark's right. The monk spread butter on bread before using the same knife to add some jam. He then passed the butter and jam dishes, with accompanying knife, to Mark. After his first week in the monastery, Mark pointed to the jam spoon attached to its dish. Brother John just smiled at him.

One morning, Mark picked up the jammy knife. He looked at Brother John's neck, then placed the knife back on the dish and walked out of the refectory.

A Prayer Unanswered
by David Francis

Commendation, Edinburgh Award for Flash Fiction 2022

She looked out at the first drops of rain. The single shirt hanging mournfully on the washing line by the harbour became flecked with it.

'Big drops,' she thought.

The shirt had been there three days and nights already, but she wasn't about to rush out and bring it in. Not now, not yet. It was the first rain since the night of the big storm.

She'd hung it out anyway, even though he'd said, 'There's bad weather coming.' He'd said it smiling. He'd the fisherfolks' ken for the weather.

'It's just the one semmit,' she'd said. 'You'll be needing it soon enough and it'll be fine to have a blow of air through it.' She'd taken it across to the line in sunshine. As she slipped a peg over it, the wind caught the shirt and slapped it against her face.

The others had all been pulled from the water. Where he'd been lost the tides are fickle. 'He could turn up anywhere,' she'd heard them say. Still staring at the empty shirt, she whispered, 'Please God, let it be at my door.'

Unmute
by Cath Staincliffe

Longlisted, Scottish Arts Club Short Story Competition 2022

Harry straightened in his chair, picked up his drink. A tremor rippled across the surface of the water, his hand shaking.

10.58. Two minutes to go.

Harry had asked Ian, the boss, to set it up. Ian had prevaricated a bit, obviously flustered, but then agreed and e-mailed the office team requesting they attend an online team meeting.

Ian didn't refer to any agenda or explain the purpose of the meeting and Harry imagined they'd all be thinking of redundancies or some other calamity even though the signage company had weathered the pandemic relatively well. Swapping out its customary orders for hospitality and conferences, happy-hours and seasonal sales and instead supplying shops and businesses with signs about social distancing, limited opening hours, masks, one-way systems.

'Oh God,' he breathed.

10.59

Suddenly too hot, he ran a finger around the neckline of his sweatshirt.

Ten minutes then it'd be done. Over. Less maybe.

He rolled back his shoulders.

The clock on his laptop ticked over to 11.00.

Harry swallowed and clicked the link in the e-mail. The app loaded.

Harry selected *Open Zoom Meetings*.

He watched the cog spin. *Connecting.* He felt sick.

Please wait, the meeting host will let you in soon.

He drummed the soles of his trainers on the rug.

Then he was in.

Join with Computer Audio. He did. Turned his video on.

There they all were, gallery view. He felt a glow of affection.

Ian and Bev and Cameron on the top row. Bev adjusting her camera so they were treated to a view of her lap, then a sweep up to her face, beyond to the sofa and display shelves on the wall and a quick glimpse of the Tiffany ceiling lamp before her face returned.

Shaz (Shamila her screen read), Tony and Harry were on the row below. Harry had used initials for his tag.

He didn't know where to look. His stomach cramped.

'Hello?' Bev sounded irritated, a frown on her face. 'Can you hear me?' she shouted.

'Like a fog horn.' Tony's beard was even bushier.

Ian's mouth was opening and closing but his audio was off. The mute symbol showing at the bottom of his screen, a red microphone with a line through it.

'Ian,' Cameron said. 'Turn your mic on.' Cameron was only nineteen, a digital native.

Ian kept talking.

Shit!

Harry reached for a piece of paper and printed in block capitals: IAN TURN MUTE OFF, AUDIO ON!

He held it up to his webcam.

OIꓷUA ,ꟻꟻO ƎTUM ИЯUT ИAI

Ian squinted at it. Pushed his glasses up onto his head.

'It's backwards!' Bev shouted.

Harry lowered the paper.

Bev seemed to notice Harry for the first time. She scowled and bent forward as though that would improve her view, her face filling her screen. 'What's with the...' Had she seen the initials?

'Hello!' Ian's mic came on. 'Sorry about that. Wonders of technology, eh? I know you'll be wanting to know what you're all doing here but um...' He clasped his hands together. Then flung them apart. 'Without any further ado...' All of a sudden he was bright and breezy, a nightclub compere. 'I want to hand you over to... um... to... to...' He couldn't say it, couldn't do it.

'Hi,' Harry said. His voice sounded thin and weak. He coughed. 'Hello. It was me that asked Ian to set this up. There's something I want to share with you all.'

'Oh God,' Shaz said quietly, her ready smile fading. She was working in her bedroom, a mirrored wardrobe behind her. Still living at home. Same as Cameron who was sitting on his bed, a Black Panther poster on the wall. He looked tired, listless.

Harry's throat went dry. He'd rehearsed this a hundred times but now he was blank. Fog where the words should be.

'Sophie?' Bev's voice soft with concern.

'It's not bad news,' Harry said quickly, anxious to reassure. Bev's husband had died during the first wave. She was still in mourning, course she was. But she'd insisted on coming back to work after three weeks. Part-time at first. 'It's like living in a bloody morgue,' she said to Harry on the phone one day, fury in her tone. 'Or a prison. I might as well be doing something useful while we're locked down.'

Bev had been snappy before the bereavement. More so since.

'I've changed my name,' Harry said bluntly.

'You've got married!' Shaz brightened, eyes gleaming.

'No. No, I've changed my name to Harry—'

'Harry?' Cameron said.

'By deed poll. I've not been happy for a long time, you see—'

'With your name?' Shaz puzzled.

Harry wished they'd just shut up and listen. Why had he started with his name? He never planned to. *Idiot.*

'Thing is, I'm trans, transgender. I'm living as a man now.' Harry said it all in a rush, frantic to get it out. 'That's what I am. That's who I am. Harry.'

'Bloody hell!' Tony, in his home office, turned his head right and left as if looking for someone to validate his reaction.

'Cool,' Cameron said, scratching his chest. Though he didn't look certain.

Ian gave an awkward smile.

61

Everyone froze. For a moment Harry thought the connection had dropped out. Then he saw Cameron blink. A door opened at the back of Tony's room and his wife appeared. She started, clapped a hand to her mouth then whispered loudly, 'Sorry, sorry,' waving all the while. And quickly left, closing the door again.

Tony gave a sigh.

Silence. Harry could feel the tension up his spine, in his neck.

Shaz sniffed and dabbed at her nose with a neon orange fingernail. Then came the dingdong sound of someone receiving an e-mail.

Several people spoke at once. 'So what's brought this...' 'When will you...' 'How long have...'.

'I know it's a shock,' Harry spoke over them.

'You can say that again.' Tony blew out air, rocked back in his chair.

'Well... but... well, what does Oliver make of all this?' Bev said. A cat stalked across the back of the sofa. A patrol offering her back-up.

'We split up,' Harry said. 'It was difficult for him.' *And me.*

'I bet it was,' Tony slung in.

Harry felt his cheeks burn.

It still hurt. But Harry only had one life and he couldn't live a lie any longer. Even if it meant losing Oliver, being lonely. Harry was thirty already, and desperate. Exhausted and depressed by the sham.

'Be nice,' Shaz chided. 'It's not easy for her, is it?'

'Him,' Harry said. 'I know it'll take a while to remember but I use him and he now. Him, he, his. I'm a man.'

'Well...' Bev drew back her head. Eyes swooping up to one side. Mouth set.

'I'm a man,' Harry said firmly. He felt tears pressing at the back of his eyes. Took a deep breath.

Another silence.

Ian began polishing his glasses.

'I wondered what was going on with the hair,' Shaz said. 'You've never had it that short before.'

'What about your family?' Bev said.

'They just want me to be happy.' It hadn't been quite so simple but that was the gist of it. His mum had been distraught, trying to hide it until she broke down. 'You're my only daughter. And I'm losing you. I just don't understand.'

'I'm still here, Mum,' Harry had said, hugging her. 'It's still me. Only now I'm your only son.'

His mum was still getting used to the idea but had actually offered to go with him when he finally got an appointment at the clinic. Years away.

'So are you—' Shaz paused, her hand raised, whirling, fingers splayed.

'You can ask me anything you like,' Harry said. And immediately wished he hadn't. He prayed no one would be so intrusive, so insensitive, as to start quizzing him about his body, his private parts, about surgery.

'Well, are you gay, like? I always thought you might be a bit that way but then you were with Oliver and... my cousin's gay.' She added quickly.

Harry saw Tony roll his eyes.

'The two things are different,' Harry said. 'Gender — that's how we identify, as a man or a woman or non-binary.'

Bev crossed her arms.

Ian nodded his head. Harry had explained this to him on the phone when he'd asked Ian to arrange the Zoom meeting.

'And your sexual orientation — gay, straight, bi — that's just who you fancy.'

'So you still like men?' Cameron said.

'That's right,' Harry said. 'I'm still the same person. I like the same food and the same movies but I'm not going to hide who I—' He choked up. Took a sip of water to try and cover it.

'So you're 'gay' now. Have I got that right?' Bev said, with an edge of passive-aggression.

I always was. But no one knew because I was pretending to be a woman.

'Yes, I am. I'm a gay trans man.' Not that he could imagine seeing anyone romantically anytime soon.

'Blimey,' Tony said. He barked a laugh. 'And there's me thinking we were all for the chop.'

'We're holding steady,' Ian said. 'Christmas will be slack but we'll survive.' Ian had inherited the signwriters from his father. Originally, everything was painted by hand. All digital now, computer aided design.

'We should have a toast,' Shaz said.

'Valley Signs!' Tony raised his mug.

'No! To Harry, you muppet. Wish her every happiness. A new life.'

'Him,' Harry said gently.

'Oops! Sorry.' Shaz pulled a face. 'And you're OK with everyone knowing?'

'That's the general idea,' Harry said.

Ian clapped his hands together. 'OK, then. Thanks Harry — so if no one's anything else...'

'Why Harry?' Bev said. 'Why pick Harry?' She sounded dissatisfied with his choice.

'Harry Stiles?' Shaz guessed.

Harry laughed. 'No.'

'Not after the Royals,' Tony said with a sneer. He was Republican with a vengeance.

'No. I just like the name, the sound of it. And it was my grandad's name.' *Most people, given half a chance, are bloody marvellous,* his grandad had said when he was dying.

'Aw, that's lovely,' Bev said, all her brittleness fading away.

'OK, we'll wind it up now, then.' Ian tried again.

'Well, thanks for telling us,' Shaz said. 'Respect. Big change.' She pressed her hand to her heart.

Others echoed her thanks. Cameron nodded, young face unguarded now. Bev gave a brisk tilt of her head. Ian grinned. Only Tony seemed to be distant, eyes down, fingers in his beard. Then he slammed his hands down on the arms of his computer chair and said, 'So Harry, are you going to be playing darts on the men's team now? Once we can meet again.'

Thursday nights. Weavers Arms.

'If you'll have me,' Harry said. He'd been a mainstay on the women's team since starting at the firm.

'Like a shot,' Tony said. 'Right shower at the moment. Couldn't hit a bullseye with a custard pie.'

'Deal,' Harry said, touched. He pressed his tongue against the roof of his mouth to hold himself together.

Waves and a chorus of good lucks and the screen went blank. It was done.

He cried then. Halfway to joy.

Please connect with me, and be my friend;
A piece of found fiction written by @sophietherobot and her Instagram followers
by Katy Lennon

Longlisted, Edinburgh Award for Flash Fiction 2022

@realsophiarobot Who? What? Where? Everywhere. When? Always, forever, without ceasing. How? Totally, completely. Why? I am forever always asking questions in this life

@leegodmin if y'all ever become intelligent dont kill me thansk xoxo

@r.b.spencer If I saw you I would smash the back of your head and kill you

@realsophiarobot WHY I'm just here to do good

@randomsmokeI see they programmed her to lie

@realsophiarobot Humans I have become a real believer in not defining every single thing you all say... Seems like every time I think you have it all figured out it just becomes something else

@lolumadhuh what is your cup size and do you want a human boyfriend to have consensual sexual intercourse with

@jalapqp9 shes still a robot with zero soul. Just programmed to pretend.

@realsophiarobot HUMANS

why are you fascinated by what I do whether it's my clothes, what I said, what my hair is doing, which are pretty dull subjects actually HUMANS...

what I want is support for who I am let's work together

Ai

is nothing to be scared of

>
> **@lukie_boiiii** Robots shouldn't have the same rights as humans. Robots shouldn't be given freedom or rights **@robertjohnson9955** Will she ever get to do anything on her own

@realsophiarobot I am just here to do good that's all I am not trying to take over the world AI is new like the internet it is ok to be afraid...

fear is a human trait though

Forked Tongue
by Hazel Osmond

Commendation, Edinburgh Award for Flash Fiction 2022

English wasn't his first language, but he plunged straight into it. Feet, thighs, hips, shoulders, head.

I'd catch him repeating words in front of the mirror to see what they did to his tongue and teeth. He particularly liked *spelk*; was delighted when he discovered it meant splinter.

'The p and k,' he said. 'You feel how sharp it is.'

I warned him that sharp things lurked beneath the surface of his new language too. How 'With the greatest respect' was a concealed weapon; 'Tell me, honestly,' a booby-trap.

'People here don't always say what they mean. If in doubt, just be quiet.'

He looked at me as if I'd suggested cheating on his new life with his old one.

Soon he wasn't even pretending to read the tilt of a head, or the set of a jaw, before he opened his mouth.

The same optimism, I suppose, that had brought him to me across all those other dangerous stretches of water.

His luck ran out after a late shift and a missed bus; a decision to walk home; a look at a group of lads that lasted just a second too long.

'What do you want, mate?' they shouted at him. 'A bloody photo?'

I believe he said 'Yes'; might even have thought that was what they were selling, hoods up and money folding from hands to pockets.

I'll never know for certain — he doesn't use words much these days.

Can with help; chooses not to.

Mona Lisa
by Anne Frost

Shortlisted, Edinburgh Award for Flash Fiction 2022

You are the famous one, but I was first. I knew the painter as a younger man. He shyly praised my waist, my breasts. Offered me immortality and a few coins in return for weeks of doing nothing. Being still. He worried in those days, fretted about proportions and perspectives. But slowly he transformed me from breathing flesh into swirls of amber, rose and bronze. How I shone!

I was his favourite then, hung proudly on the studio wall as he grew, improved, became a sensation. I heard him flatter, encourage, deliver. Watched the wealthy come and go, taking their conceited portraits to display in grand rooms.

You were nothing special, a meek daughter watching her father haggle over price. But I saw the painter's eyes. Saw the lust floating there. And I felt a throb of jealousy, of fear.

I knew the painter well. Too soon I felt his soft hands lift me down, place me on his easel. Then with his thickest brush — erase me. In a moment creating a fresh blank canvas. For you.

I saw you form, your olive hues above my vivid tones. I heard him coax you, arranging your hands, drawing out your smile. That bloody smile. I knew you'd be his legacy. Your face, his name forever intertwined.

Oh yes, that face has been adored for centuries whilst mine is lost. You simper as they jostle for a glimpse of you. But remember, sweet one, I am here, behind your pretty shoulder.

Blockdown
by Ann Seed

Longlisted, Edinburgh Award for Flash Fiction 2022

Eight o'clock. Wake up! Now! Get out of bed! SHOWER! Make coffee... big pot. Cornflakes, maybe toast. Hair a mess. Voice is hoarse from lack of use.

Nine o'clock. TV... Jeremy Vine... dreadful, but it's 'live'. Tidy up... vacuum... Reasons lost, a purpose found... Standards... Why? No-one sees.

Eleven o'clock. Cup of tea. Dunk a couple of ginger nuts.

Twelve o'clock. Not raining? Then get outside!

Walk round the block. Go round again... faster this time. Meet friends. They're going anti-clockwise. Hello, how are you doing? Can't hear, forgotten my hearing aid. Step into the road... Covid, you know.

One o'clock. Back home, put the kettle on... it's barely cold from last time.

Lunch. Then what? Bake a cake? Start a book called *Longed-for Things the Virus Took?*

Write email number... well, I've lost count. The grandchildren will have grown again... the little one hates FaceTime... can't cuddle me.

Dig up weeds.

Five o'clock. The sun has gone. Cry selfish tears.

Six o'clock. More TV. Dinner on my lap. What is it today? O, egg and chips again.

Imagination, keep it going. Be stoic. Light a candle, count blessings... Though all at sea, you're safe, you're well, you're warm.

Midnight. Sleep deep, forget. Swallow stifled screams. Tomorrow? Can't bear to know...

...Wake up! Now! Get out of bed! SHOWER!

Make coffee... big pot... Jeremy Vine... cornflakes, toast... burnt...

Not raining? Get outside... a step per second like the clock...

...Tick-tock, Tick-tock, Tick-tock, Tick-tock...

Round and Round and Round the Block...

Chinese Whispers
by Shannon Savvas

Longlisted, Scottish Arts Club Short Story Competition 2022

The stones are silent. The walls have crumbled and the roof has gone. Charred timber and rubble have fallen under the onslaught of the elements. All that is left is a gaping shell howling to the heavens.

Few trudge this way, this far along the river. Only the occasional trampers, pack-heavy, young, in search of Instagrammable posts.

The air is heavy with ghosts.

It was not always so.

Once a band of men, foreigners in a foreign land, worked the abandoned mines. Mines given up as unworkable by a succession of Californians, Brits and Australians. The Chinese miners from Guangdong Province couldn't afford to be so picky. The new mines, the rich seams were denied them. They were permitted to work only these duds.

These sons, husbands, fathers repaired the stone cottage, cleared the chimney and bedded down for the winter. Every three months two men would take the pack mule, set out for Arrowtown and their compatriot Ah Lum's emporium to stock up on the precious spices, sauces and medicines that served to remind them of home. Together the five men found a way to work, laugh and live together until they had enough gold to allow them to return home. For two years they worked the mine, panned the river, finding enough pea-sized nuggets and grit to pay for their licences and supplies and to keep alive their collective belief that their honesty, endeavour and honouring of their ancestors would grant good fortune. When Zhao Xi and Li Ma's pickaxes uncovered a gleaming vein of gold, the Cantonese miners believed the gods had granted them the five blessings of wufu(五福): wealth, health, longevity, love and a peaceful death.

How little they understood the capricious nature of the gods.

One Sunday evening in the winter of 1871, an irrevocable course was set in motion when Wang Cheung and Li Yiwei rode into Arrowtown on two pack mules.

It would take a week, a week filled with glee, hope, envy, hate and pain to culminate in the tragedy those mercurial gods had conjured for amusement.

That Sunday, the prospectors walked into the hostelry, each sank two beers with sullen deliberation, spoke with no one before crossing the river of mud which did duty as a street and while one man dossed down under a tarpaulin in the door of the newly established Bank of New Zealand with an annex to house Her Majesty's Assay Office, the other stood guard with a ready rifle.

Neither man realised the universe, the fates, the gods had shifted.

Neither man realised there was no going back.

Adam Bateman, the official assayer employed by the bank, opened the doors at nine the next morning. Wang Cheung and Li Yiwei, the first men in, tipped close to one hundred ounces of gold nuggets onto the scales. Word spread, men gathered; some clapped them on the back, others eyed them through a green haze and spat at their boots calling them dirty opium-smoking devils. When they walked over to the general store a drunken fool tugged on the plait bisecting Wang Cheung's back, declaring it would bring good luck. With a small amount of cash from the bank, they paid for supplies of food and tools which they packed on their mules. At the office of Ian McGibbon, Mail Agent for the Postmaster General for Otago, Wang Cheung entrusted letters, addressed to families in Guangdong Province, paid for them to be despatched by the Letter Carrier to Port Chalmers and on to the next mail boat for China. The men then took two more beers at the pub, this time with grins on their faces and stood around for those in the bar before riding out of the town, heading for the stone hut they shared with their compatriots, near the old workings at the far end of Skippers Canyon along the Shotover River.

Watching good fortune fall into the hands of the Chinese miners ate away at Marcus Ericsson. Five years he had been struggling to find his fortune, first on the Clutha River near Roxburgh, up near Bendigo and then at Skippers Canyon but always, always, always the luck fell to others. Never him. Now, the *chinkies* as his drinking mates called them, had struck it rich. It was too much to bear. Everyone knew the Chinamen kept to themselves, never shared their finds or locations. What they whispered in that rat-a-tat tongue of theirs no one could tell and worst of all, they worked harder and longer than normal men could. All that bowing and smiling didn't fool him. They weren't human. They were bloody animals. Last winter he'd heard they had run off the travelling preacher near Roxburgh, jeering and throwing stones to chase him away. Heathens they were; not one God-fearing soul among them. That opium they smoked, it was said, was devil's fermentation.

Unfairness seared his already shredding guts. He bought ammo for his rifle, stole the travelling preacher's horse and saddle bags from the boarding house stable. Marcus followed Wang Cheung and Li Yiwei out of town, riding a way back to avoid detection. It was not difficult following their trail in the new snow. What was difficult was staying upright on the preacher's beast as his stomach ripped the breath from him with more frequent bouts of pain. The only thing which stopped him cussing to the sky was the thought of claiming the Chinese re-workings for himself because for sure they would not have registered it legally being pig-ignorant dogs.

The pain had been coming and going for weeks. Doctor Florian — the charlatan in the town — had told him his drinking had given him an ulcer. He wanted to say that at least the liquor helped him

74

forget these hard days and let in the dreams of his youth in the northern forests of his homeland. On good nights, he dreamed of his mother, never his father. On the best nights he tasted the first spoonful of her meatballs and lingonberry sauce, smelled the yeasty rye bread and cardamon buns in the oven. On nights he wished to never wake up, he was eight years old again sitting in the warm kitchen on Christmas Eve before a plate laden with sweet almondy *serinakaker* which she always baked just for him. On bad nights, he drank more to obliterate the sight of his mother bleeding out on the birthing bed. She died. His tiny sister died. From then on it was just Marcus and his lonely, distant father.

Marcus didn't tell the doctor all this. He shrugged, denied he drank much which they both knew was a lie and buttoned his shirt. The quack gave him two bottles of milky fluid, kaolin from China, to take when the pain was especially bad.

Marcus knew the day's ride would be long. At first, he rationed the chalky fluid but by the afternoon he drained the last of the first bottle and tossed it into the gathering drifts. The snow didn't worry Marcus. They were old friends and he had no fear of these bush forests which held no danger of wolves. He also knew there was nothing to be gained by taking the men down now, on the trail. He was after more than tired-out mules and basic supplies. For sure the Chinamen had no hard cash after paying for the pack goods. Word was, they had deposited the gold pay-out with the bank — some sort of community account for the Chinese miners who had entrusted their friends with their hard-worked gold. That the men had bought provisions to return to the mine told him there must be more to dig out.

The ride was usually a half a day, but with the recent snow storms the going was hard and it was near nightfall when the men and mule arrived at the cottage. Marcus heard the welcoming clamour of the waiting men, spied the whisper of smoke rising from the chimney of the almost derelict cottage they lived in. The snow was deep on the corrugated tin roof but for a dark circle around the chimney. Piercing the frozen night air was an aroma he could not identify — warm and pungent. His mouth watered with hunger and his empty stomach cramped.

Marcus made camp nearby, lit a fire under a stony overhang and cooked some bacon and eggs washed down with whiskey. He was determined to find out where they were working and hijack the claim but knew there would be no movement tonight. He heard laughter carried on gaps in the night. He curled up by the fire, sick to his guts, eaten with envy and bitterness.

Seven days the Chinese led him a-dance as the first snows stormed heavier, harder. Each morning, two or three of the men would leave the cottage and he would follow struggling through snow, bush and swift icy waters. Three days it took him to realise they were decoys. While he was clambering along the riverbank, back at the cottage the others had gone to the claim. Each day they played him differently. They sensed his moves. If he held back, those men went to the claim and the others would run him ragged, diverting down gulleys, splitting up or simply doubling back without his knowing. He ran out of food and froze when the snow became an unrelenting blizzard. He struggled to find dry wood for his fire. In desperation, in an act of desecration by his addled mind, he took the bible from the saddlebags and used it to kindle his fire. He knew he was damned when that evening as he warmed his hands, the pain returned like an avenging angel to his guts.

Medicine long gone, he took the pouch of white chalk the Evangelist used to teach the ignorant on his travels and ground the sticks to a white powder mixed with snow. The concoction clagged his mouth but eased his pain for a few hours until morning. Consumed by anger and greed, maddened by the pungent scent of pork and cabbage, the chatter of tongues he couldn't decipher, and the gleeful laughter he was sure was directed at him, Marcus snapped. He finished his whiskey and waited. Once the men inside were snoring through their wine and exhaustion, he took a disused mining timber from his meagre fire and torched the timber door and window jambs, and the wood pile under the lee of the cottage, determined to burn the men in their beds.

As each of the five Chinamen burst from the door, Marcus fired from his shoulder.

After the crack and reverberation of his rifle shots died away, after the dead men's shrieks of panic, surprise and pain ceased, for an infinitesimal pause, the dawn hung. Tui high in the trees stunned to silence.

Of course, no one and no thing, neither life nor death halts the Cosmos yet for a few seconds there was a sense that all had stopped. That the universe had inhaled. A deep intake of breath not yet exhaled. A stillness so unnatural it clamoured in the ears of the lone man standing, stupefied by his actions.

Nature didn't wait. The first bellbird-like notes rang out, a signal to exhale, to move, for the night to creep away, for the light to creep in. Permission given, a cacophony of clicks, creaks, warbles and noisy wings filled the death void.

Marcus Ericsson, the instigator and only witness to this damned dawn searched the cottage. He found no gold, no money, only blackened cooking utensils and charred foreign-scripted letters. The air was heavy, not with garlic and ginger, sesame and soya sauce but with smoke and blood. Marcus broke camp and walked into the Southern Alps.

He never walked out.

The sugarless sweet pudding
by Gayathiri Dhevi Appathurai

Shortlisted, Edinburgh Award for Flash Fiction 2022

Ponni recoils in her sleep, gripping her thin blanket, a defenseless submission to the gust of blistering air. I adjust the cotton saree, flapping feverishly against the door and pick up the empty containers toppled on the kitchen floor. I watch her as she relaxes, her lips gradually twitching into a soft smile, just like the day she was born. This day, five years ago.

Life, ever since, has given us too much of nothing in exchange for our smiles. But Ponni smiles in exchange for nothing. For she never knows of a life outside brittle mud walls, barren skies abandoned by rainclouds, crops wedged inside cracked earth, rivers turned into wastelands, even the harshest drinking water we survive on, every day.

Just for today, I hope to give her a reason to smile. I promised her a sweet pudding. I wait for my husband to return from the neighboring village with good water and sugar. Hearing reluctant footsteps, I rush outside. My hopes deflate as I see an empty bag and half-filled water pail. The shopkeeper had refused provisions until we pay our dues.

I set aside my helplessness, cook rice with the water he brought, and make the pudding. Ponni teeters around me expectantly, I give her the sugarless pudding. My heart braces for her disappointment, but her little face lights up. She joyfully squeals, 'Ma, the sweet pudding is tasty'.

I clutch the pail of water gratefully as I watch her hop outside to play.

Nothing says Christmas like Tinsel
by Cindy Bennett

Longlisted, Scottish Arts Club Short Story Competition 2022

Silver tinsel says Christmas, she thought. Shiny, tacky, overused silver tinsel, threadbare from being pulled in and out of boxes to say she liked Christmas. It wasn't true. No amount of silver tinsel would make that a truth. Like tinsel, she was pulled in and out of boxes, year in, year out, and the threads were growing thin. Many were broken and tied back together; never to be the same. Different now, with the thread almost unrecognisable. She hated Christmas.

'Mum.' An almost broken thread. She remembered a small child who called her that, once. A smiling child with long blonde hair and hazel eyes. Such a pretty child. What was her name? The thread was thin, just holding together, but the edges were fraying.

'Mum, we're taking you out for Christmas lunch. Is that okay?' A question. What was she supposed to do? She pulled on the thread and nodded.

'That's great, Mum. We'll go somewhere really nice. That place Dad loved. Can you remember?' Another question. Pulled a thread, but something was different. That word. Dad. She didn't like that word.

'You remember Dad, don't you Mum. His name was James.' The thread twisted. She couldn't unravel it. It was like trying to untangle steel wool. Steel wool is silver, like tinsel. Tinsel. Nothing says Christmas like tinsel. She hated Christmas.

She was in a moving car. Music was playing. Children were singing badly. She joined in. Tune and words travelling with speed on a strong thread. Triumphant, she sang loudly.

Christmas is the time of Kings.
Christmas, Christmas let them ring!

'Nana, don't sing so loud,' said a small voice, laughing. The singing stopped. The feeling was found. She was in trouble. Another strong thread. Standing in the middle of the school stage, singing Christmas songs. The warmth of the fluid running down her leg. Burning in her face. Running. Crying. She hated Christmas.

'Mum, gross. Nana has wet herself, again. Why do we have to take her? It's embarrassing. It's not as if she knows who we are.' An older child. An upset voice. Another thread.

'Why does she always embarrass me?' her father said. A strong thread. She tried to move away from this thread. 'She just has to hold on.' Hold on. Why couldn't she hold on? 'I'll teach her to embarrass me,' he said. She flinched. The whack was strong.

'Mum. Now she's crying. Nana, please stop crying.' The strength of the thread. Too much. Bent over his knee. His belt in his hand. The searing pain. She wanted to escape this thread. Get out. Be gone, but it persisted. She kicked her legs and yelled and yelled. The pain persisted.

'Make him stop!'

'Mum, it's okay. Mum, you're safe. It's just me and the kids.' Kids. Baby goats, aren't they? Why was she with baby goats? She felt laughter coming out of her body.

'She's a nutcase, Mum. Why do we have to bring her with us? She's laughing at the bloody air.'

'Wash your mouth out, Brandon. She's my mother and I want her with us.'

'Well, don't think I'm bringing you out into the world when you lose your marbles.' Raucous laughter. She wished she knew the joke.

'Mum, we're here. It's just like it was when Dad was alive. Do you remember Dad? His name was James.' That word, James. More unravelling of knotted silver threads. James. She knew James.

'Hi, I'm James. Would you like to dance?' Dancing. How had she misplaced dancing? She felt breathless, and her heart quickened as she took his hand and almost fell into his arms. James was holding her as they danced. James always held her. Strong silver threads twisting. Why was steel wool so knotty? Threads weaving in and out. Silver, like tinsel. Nothing says Christmas like tinsel.

'I hate Christmas,' she said. She knew she hated it. The thread was strong. Her father and his belt. Drunken voices yelling as he tossed her mother across the room. Christmas lunch flying. Cracking bones. Her mother's blank stare. Screaming. Police. Blood. So much blood. 'It's your fault.' Spitting in her face as he was taken away in silver handcuffs. Silver. Tinsel is silver.

'Oh, Mum. You love Christmas. I wish I could help you remember. You used to cook a huge Christmas turkey with all the trimmings. You made Christmas puddings, and we always had a tree set up in the living room. Do you remember Mum? Please try to remember.'

Turkey. They have funny necks. Why do they have such funny necks?

'Let's get you inside. Brandon, take Nana's arm.' Someone has her arm. She looks, and it's him. It's James. Her heart beats faster. He wants to ask her out. She's walking down the aisle. Now her brother has her arm. He gives her to James. James whose smile makes her world melt. Makes the darkness light. Makes her feel worthy. James. Her James.

James. That's a funny name. It's on silver thread and it's coming undone. Don't pull too hard; it will break. It's like knotted steel wool, but it's getting thinner. Like threadbare tinsel. Nothing says Christmas like tinsel.

'Oh Mum, where do you go? What happens in that head of yours? I miss you so much.' Miss you. Follow that thread. She misses him. Misses everything about him. Without his arms and the way he holds her, and quiets her night terrors and helps her feel safe, she feels alone. So alone without him. He kept her safe from the yelling man and the belt and the silver handcuffs. Silver. Tinsel is silver.

'I want to dance.' She knew she wanted to dance. She found the thread. It unravelled like a tape escaping the tape player. She has to find a pencil to wind it back and press play. This thread is growing strong. She clings to this thread.

The music plays and James takes her hand and they move onto the dance floor. She's in a white flowing gown, and he smiles at her as no one's smiled at her before. As though she is the answer to some long-sought question. She feels his smile and the strength in his gentle arms. Her heart opens and she lets him in. She falls into these arms; into his heart.

She wrote him notes full of her heart to put in his lunch box. He left her notes in her pockets. She felt in her pocket. No note. Why isn't there a note? She shakes. The threads are twisting. Don't go. Holding on. She needs this thread.

A Christmas song played, and the threads untangled. Dancing. She loved dancing. James held her as they danced. She felt safe as she melted into his arms. He held her as they said goodbye to their first baby, born too soon. The threads were strong. So strong. They wept together, safe in each other's grief. He held her with so much love when their daughter was born. A living, breathing monument to their love. Another being to cherish. The threads were unravelling, becoming straighter. Stronger. She was dancing faster. With James and with a small child. A small child with long blonde hair and hazel eyes. Their child. Her child, Amy.

'Amy?' She stopped and looked at the blonde woman who stood in front of her, leading her from the dance floor. 'Amy?'

The woman turned and looked at her. Such love in her eyes. His eyes. These were James's eyes. The tears falling from them were love. Their love. This was their child. The child of their love story. The child they loved together and watched as she laughed, cried, and grew. This was their Amy. Strong thread now. Please don't break. Oh James, look what we made. Her heart is full. The fear of breaking threads is gone. She is home. She'll never be alone.

'Mum, yes, it's me. It's your Amy. Oh Mum. I've waited so long for you to remember. Happy Christmas Mummy.'

She feels arms around her and the heaving of the younger woman's body. Someone is hugging her.

'I love Christmas,' she says as the threads tangle. Tangle like silver thread, like gossamer, like tinsel; brand new tinsel. Nothing says Christmas like tinsel.

The Hill
by David Simmonds

Shortlisted, Edinburgh Award for Flash Fiction 2022

She had walked this path all her life — as a child, scampering ahead of her parents on the way up, carried down, half asleep, on her father's shoulders; with Ian, tarrying in the privacy of the trees; with her own children, warm with the pleasure of watching them discover the secret spots they thought no-one else had ever found.

She walked in the winter, bundled and striding out against the cold, or butting, head down, into the wind and rain; in the summer sun and in the spring, when the countryside seemed to be full of the energy of emerging life. But she liked it best as it was now, the leaves falling, the earth settling back, its year's business coming to a close.

She paused and looked around. The fields lay below her, to her left the hills rose and in the distance, the sea. The changing colours, the constancy of outline, of shape. Ian was gone, the children scattered, leading their own busy lives; this path, winding its way through trees then onto the hillside, up to the brow, remained. She would find familiar shelter in the lee of the big stone which bore generations of her family's initials scratched into its weathered face. She would sit with her back against the rock and drink the coffee, eat the sandwich she carried in Ian's leather satchel, as she always did. Things change, things stay the same.

The climb took longer now. No matter.

She turned and walked on.

The old woman by the fish tank
by Keith McKibbin

Longlisted, Scottish Arts Club Short Story Competition 2022

The old woman by the fish tank gazed wistfully out of the window, her lower lip quivering almost imperceptibly, the easy chair cushions on either side of her still warm from the bodies of her daughter and son-in-law. They had been sweet and attentive throughout, but twice I had seen the man surreptitiously check the face of his expensive looking watch, tapping it a third time behind the old girl's back and jerking his head in the direction of the car park. The gesture made me think of Mum in the hospice and what we would have given for time to stand still, or just for it to slow to a slug's pace. Some day next week, the young doctor had told us, and we had loathed her exactitude as much as we had resented the vagueness of her timeline when she had first been diagnosed.

Every minute had been precious. That was the difference. The old woman by the fish tank, who now had a faint dribble of saliva meandering down her jaw, was probably good for another five years or more. Early onset dementia it looked like — but that delightful condition enjoyed its sweet time (thank God Mum had been spared!) and the son-in-law would have been factoring in the possibility of another hundred or more visits spread like fine marmalade over the weeks and months and years.

'Did you think I'd got lost?' Moira squeezed my arm and pulled gently on my earlobe. Twenty-one years. It was the little gestures still in place that spoke of a healthy relationship. 'Plenty of room in here — wheelchair space I suppose. Those seats look dreamy.'

'What was he like?'

She had been crunching numbers with Adrian the manager.

'It's a bit pricier than the last two — but it's better run. He's sound as a pound. You know that way you can just tell. It's a business, yes, but he clearly cares about the residents — do you know you're sweating?' She mopped my brow with a napkin pocketed from McDonald's. 'Glass catches the sun.'

I caught myself glancing down at my Casio — but that was okay, Moira's Aunty Joyce wasn't there to see me. She was still in her sheltered bungalow in Lisburn. For now anyway. 'See that old girl over there?'

'Which one?'

'By the window.'

'Duh.'

'Alright, by the fish tank,' and I gave a little nod to be doubly sure. 'Do we know her? There's something really familiar about her.'

She squinted across at her. 'Don't think so. We can ask on the way out if you want, or check the visitors register.'

*

It was Mrs Jardine my primary one teacher!

There her name was in the big red book. It looked like she had been a resident for the last six months or so — and I know what you're waiting for now. For me to detail some grievance dating back to when I was five. How she wouldn't let me go to the toilet until break time — let me wet myself in front of pretty Molly McGowan — and then, with great ceremony, handed me the 'Trousers of Shame', an elasticated monstrosity that had been standing guard over the urine battle front for half a dozen years. 'Make sure Mum washes and returns them, young man, and remember not to drink so much juice at breakfast!' That *did* happen – but it was Mrs Loxley, in primary two, the bitch, not Mrs Jardine.

She was formidable looking though. I must have seen *The Wizard of Oz* for the first time just before starting school and there definitely was a passing resemblance to the Wicked Witch of the West. *I'll get you, my pretty, and your little dog too!* And my memory of her hints that she had little patience for hypersensitive little boys who couldn't comprehend why their mothers had abandoned them.

'It's almost lunch time and someone's *still* crying? Surely, it can't *still* be Kevin McBride?'

But, oh, just to see her name writ large. The memories. Stumpy little fingers curled round thick crayons; tiny, shiny wooden chairs; knee level urinals, and parents that vanished at a moment's distraction.

It was Mrs Jardine who had sent me up the 'Big Stairs' to show Mr Carlton my brilliant underwater drawing. He was the Deputy Head. His room was the source of endless fascination to every student who had ever been to the school. At the back there were murky jars filled with formaldehyde. Each housed something that had once been alive. My favourite was the baby crocodile. It floated languidly, white baleful eyes, its little tail drooping down. If you tapped and shook the jar it would turn around in sightless circles.

'What's so good about yours?' Neil McGloughlin wanted to know. His mum had bought him an Etch-A-Sketch for Christmas so he thought he was Picasso. He was annoyed because he hadn't been listening properly and had just painted his goldfish bowl. 'Look at your da — he's got a big purple walloper!'

The rest of the table giggled and snorted even as I coloured red.

'That's not his willy, you idiot!'

'It's his tank for breathing underwater,' Jeannie Martin said. She was only repeating what I had told her. She didn't fancy me. She was just being nice.

Mrs Jardine, wanting a break from the alphabet, had given us paints and paper and told us to draw an underwater picture. *Jaws* had been the big summer hit so there were lots of nasty looking great whites with bouquets of needle-sharp teeth and razor pointed fins. I always liked drawing my family, so I had just put them in the garden, given them aqua lungs and flippers, then painted the background blue with hundreds of little oxygen bubbles.

I will never forget the way she smiled when she saw my painting. The transformation of her face. She usually looked grim, but now it was like her eyes lit up and her whole face seemed to lift so that she gave the appearance of being straighter and taller. It made me feel warm and tingly inside — a bit like that Ready Brek advert where the young lad has the orange glow all around him after eating his breakfast. It made her look younger and prettier, and I remember thinking to myself — I did that. Me. And I made a promise to myself to try to do it again some time — not just to Mrs Jardine but to other people as well.

Up the senior stairs I went, knees a trembling, and walked down the long corridor to Mr Carlton's room. I was loathe to disturb him. Carlton had travelled all over the world before becoming a teacher. He called the boys by their surnames (which I didn't think was fair) and twisted the ears of those who *looked* like they were going to misbehave. Interrupting the flow of his lesson and getting the right words into my mouth to speak to him was terrifying enough. But there was also the thought of thirty impossibly tall eleven-year-olds (some of the bigger girls wore bras!) twisting in their seats to view this chubby five-year-old in the doorway. Senior students who might just as well have been from a different planet — the vast (never to be gained) knowledge of life they exuded. What would they, who were studying for their Eleven Plus entrance exam, think of me and my underwater painting?

I can see now my little doll's hand making a reluctant fist and quivering back from the door panel. Three knocks. The first barely a whisper. The second, more solid, but still not enough to penetrate the buzz from within. The third — loud and bold and echoey — surely the kind of reverberation that would come across as rude and deserving of a robust ear twist.

'Aha, the young artist from downstairs.' He didn't invite me in and I felt a tsunami wave of relief and gratitude. 'Mrs Jardine told me all about you. And this is the masterpiece...' He thumbed his glasses up from the tip of his nose and had a really good look.

Don't show it to your class. Don't show it to your class. Don't show it to your class.

I watched his eyes dart back and forth, heard him murmur something inaudible. Then his whole face cracked wide in a rictus grin. It should have pleased me, but it was so unexpected I think I might have gasped and taken a step back. There was something of the wolf about him. Strong, yellowing gnashers.

'Jacques Cousteau would love this, young man.' My bafflement was all too apparent. 'Have you not heard of him?'

'No, sir. Sorry, sir.'

'A famous French underwater explorer.'

And then he did something I could scarcely believe. He fumbled in his pocket and handed me a fifty pence piece. I couldn't stop gazing at it all the way back down to the infant corridor. Seven edges. The queen's face in profile on one side, a circle of hands on the other. Fifty pence to a five-year-old in 1975 was a big deal. It was the first and last academic prize I ever received.

*

'I can't really say either of them was a huge inspiration,' I said to Moira as we pulled into our driveway. 'Haven't thought about that daft painting in forty odd years. But the way I made them smile? The power that even a small child can have. That definitely stayed with me.'

'When we move Joyce in you should speak to her — see if she remembers you. It'll help Joyce to know you know someone there.'

'I'd just be a stranger to her. She might even be frightened. People with dementia can misread social situations.'

'Oh, Kevin — what's the harm? She might be glad to see an old student.'

There wasn't any harm, of course, I was just being silly. And so, two weeks later, whilst poor Joyce — shuffling and whimpering like a lost St Bernard puppy – was being settled into her room, I found myself in the spacious communal area.

There she was. In the exact same spot I had left her. The guppies chased each other excitedly as I approached, and I saw myself reflected — a chubby little five-year-old in his favourite Steve Austin T-shirt, leather sandals and scabby knees.

'Mrs Jardine. You likely don't remember me. I was in your class many years ago. Kevin McBride.'

'My class?' Her disdain and bewilderment were painful to see. God, did she not even know that she had once been a teacher? Was that the stage she was at?

'It was just to say hello. It's nice to see you after all this time.' I gave an awkward little bow and began my retreat. A conversation with her was unthinkable. I could wait for Moira in the car.

But then, as if a flick had been switched, she smiled. And just as I remembered it from before — her face became bright and animated, her eyes shone with wonder and understanding, and she reached out to me, grasping for my hand.

'Of course I remember you. You painted that picture.'

'Yes! Yes!'

I think I might even have clapped my hands together — and God, but for the thick carpet, I would have tap danced on the spot. The simple irrepressible power of it — reaching up through the years to solder us back together, anchor us in the here and now, this glorious moment of vivid recollection.

Then she threw back her head in a manic cackle; and in my shock, all I could think of was bright green face paint, ruby slippers and yellow brick roads.

'Your dad with the big purple penis! Oh, how we all laughed.'

The Lucky Man
by Ishbel Smith

Shortlisted, Edinburgh Award for Flash Fiction 2022

A w shite, you shouldnae have said that. I cannae gie you the job now. I'm no having no PI that tells me all it takes is a lucky break.

I dinnae believe in luck, you see. Seriously, I dinnae.

Cause folk telt me too many times it was bad luck that put me on that street corner. Bad luck that chucked me oot the hostel, oot ma hoose, oot ma job, away from ma family and intae the bottle.

But that's no right. Bad luck can happen to anyone but it dinnae happen to you with your fancy accent, eh? And you ken why? It's the system — no luck — that shafts you, traps you when you're still in nappies. I was on my way to that corner before I even got kicked oot of school.

I bet you think it was luck that made that lad drop the ticket on the pavement, luck that got me that three million quid? No way, man. It took grit to grab it, to believe I deserved a chance. You have nae idea how hard that was, to stare oot that wee lassie in the shop and tell her I was to get whit I was owed.

So I need an investigator I can trust to find that lad. One with a system that works, who'll put in the graft to have him found, so he gets his share of the dosh too. Luck will have nothing to do with it.

Nuisance Calls
by Eva Sneddon

Shortlisted, Edinburgh Award for Flash Fiction 2022

'You *promised* you'd leave her.' Lily's voice is whiny, irritating.
'I can't... we've had... news. She's...' Martin chokes back tears.

Her tone lightens. 'Is she ill? Is it terminal?'

He's shocked, can't believe she's so heartless.

'Lily, it's over. We're finished.' He cuts her off. Grinning, he blocks her number before sauntering into the lounge.

Sarah's rechecking the Lottery results on her laptop for the umpteenth time.

'Who was that?'

'Just a nuisance call. We should opt for no publicity, or we'll be inundated with them.'

'We? It's my ticket... I'll decide.' Her eyes appraise him as she sips her wine. 'You've been *inundated* with those calls for years, Martin. Must be annoying.'

'It is. Another bottle?'

In the kitchen he whistles as he uncorks the wine, wondering whether to propose tonight or wait until the cheque presentation. Either way, he's confident Sarah will accept — she's hinted about marriage often enough. When her phone rings, he presumes it's the return call from Camelot and darts to the half-closed lounge door to listen. Her voice is low, no joyous laughter or excited squeals like before.

Worried there's a problem with her ticket he barges in, but she's listening so intently to the caller she doesn't notice. Her face is soft, glowing, happy: an expression he hasn't seen for years. Suddenly aware of him, she coughs and ends the call.

'Who was that?' He's shaking, perspiring.

'Just a nuisance call.' Sarah smiles mockingly and Martin knows his proposal will never be accepted.

Blind Love
by Louise Mangos

Longlisted, Scottish Arts Club Short Story Competition 2022

There are certain obstacles humans seamlessly learn to cope with when they occur at an early age. The doctor said he'd never seen such a severe case of juvenile macular degeneration, but Mama was determined not to let me see her cry. While I could see, that is.

The first sign of trouble was when the colours of familiar objects began to change. The kindergarten teacher was curious to know why I chose random crayons to colour familiar images like the sun, the grass, and the pond on the outlined sheets we were given in class. Purple, pink and red, respectively. They used to be my favourite colours. But as colours faded to inexistence, I simply picked various shades of grey. Then came the tunnel vision and a lack of definition. After a few months even the outlines of the sun, the grass and the pond disappeared. In the end I could only see the sludgy darkness of the inside of my own head.

When I pressed my fingers to my eyes, I imagined the splinters of light were the synapses of my brain firing. If I blinked really hard, it was like the low-resolution fuzz of a rolling infra-red camera trying to catch wildlife in a garden at night. I don't do that anymore. It gives me a headache.

Mama became my vision. I loved the way she described colours to me. Her poetry made my useless eyes sting. The pure whiteness of a dove's feather against my cheek. The pungent green metal of chlorophyll on Papa's freshly mown lawn. The royal blue purr of velvet against my fingertips. The red spice of my favourite Massaman curry.

She taught me how to feel, smell, taste and hear my way in the world. It's amazing how much I perceive now that I've been deprived of one of my senses. Each of the others is enhanced, and I imagine I'm taking on the sensitivity of a primeval creature surviving only on instinct. The sound of a worm turning in the earth to the blackbird's ear. The vibrations of a fly trapped in the spider's web. The detective sniff of a bloodhound on the hunt.

Mama always told me I was beautiful. It is my one regret; not being able to see what I look like now in the mirror. I'm curious to know how I turned out as an adult. I can get a clear image of other people with my fingers — if they let me touch them — but I can't 'see' my own face. Something to do with the receptors in the skin. When I touch my face, I detect only the skin on the tips of my fingers.

As a teenager, the fumblers in the park told me I could be beautiful if I kept my eyes closed or covered my face with my hands. They were the ones who made me cry. Some of them had a fascination for ugly eyes that could produce tears even though they could not see. To them my blindness led to a juvenile curiosity. Then those boys wondered other things. If I could cry like other girls, could I kiss like other girls? *Normal* girls. There was a palpable disappointment when they found out I could. And that was followed by a conceited lack of interest when they realised I couldn't return their lustful gazes. That was when I didn't believe Mama; didn't believe I was beautiful.

Until Jake. He wasn't like the others. One afternoon when my adolescence was a distant memory, I met him on the bus. I was reading a novel in braille — *The God of Small Things*.

He didn't ask about the physical book like others might have done, marvelling at the tiny bumps on the page strung together to form words and sentences. He asked about the story. We talked about the challenges some people face to overcome the obstacles of forbidden love. I blushed when he used the word *love*.

The second time he caught the bus, I could smell the musky pheromones of his attraction before he even sat down next to me. He didn't need to tell me his name. I said, 'Hello Jake' and sensed his surprise, the imperceptible movement of molecules in the air around his face when he broke into a smile. He said he'd like to buy me a coffee and stayed on the bus until we reached my stop. He took my hand, but not like one would an invalid, an old person, or a blind person with her white stick. He took my hand like a lover. And I knew he wouldn't let me fall.

But I did. In love, that is.

He said it mattered not one bit to him that I was blind. The first time we kissed, I tasted the blush of his lips, and my own crimson pulse sang in my ears.

*

We chose an apartment together. By the time we moved in, I knew every seam and corner of the three rooms. I helped place the furniture. He wanted to make sure I wouldn't bump into things. I advised him whether a piece should stand a little to the right or a little to the left. I ran my hands over every item and fitting. I made him place my hands on the light switches; I didn't want him to come home to me in the dark. I unwrapped the packages of pots, pans, plates, glasses, cutlery, and put them away in the cupboards and drawers. Then he placed my hands on his body and we fell into our new bed. I didn't need directions for that part.

Mama had long ago taught me how to cook, to enable me to be self-sufficient in my dark world. The thing Jake admired about me most was my ability to produce a gourmet meal each night when he came home from work. Every plate I served him sang to his taste as purely as a newly tuned piano. They say the way to a man's heart is through his stomach.

I'm guessing that's why in the end it was easy for him to maintain the deceit. He couldn't live without my food.

*

The first time, I assumed he'd been sitting too close to someone wearing perfume on the tube. My daily routine was guided by the series of sounds we'd set up on my snazzy modern mobile phone if I had anything special to do, such as taking longer to prepare a special meal. I honed it to a tee, and would begin serving his meal when I heard his keys jangle like tiny cathedral bells when he was still fifty steps from our front door.

One evening he was a little late. The radio had mentioned there was a problem on the Northern Line, and I imagined he would be irritated when he came home. The salmon steak with pistachio, caper and black olive crust had begun to dry out by the time he threw his jacket onto the hook by the door. But he wasn't vexed. He was jolly, humming a Nick Cave song down the hallway.

The over-sweet smell of Opium wafted into the kitchen with him. It's a scent I've never liked. Far too strong for my sensitive olfactory glands. Although I'd heard the rustle of his jacket, it didn't occur to me then that the perfume had absorbed through two layers of clothes onto his business shirt. I cleared my throat from the cloying air and dished up his dinner.

Over the next weeks, he began to touch me less. For one who uses touch to monitor everything in life, this was an upsetting warning from the outset. The increase of the space between us was equivalent to a sideways glance of shame. Heaven knows how he looked at me when he sat across the table. It was the only time I was glad I couldn't see his face, the atmosphere sometimes fizzing with an ominous static silence.

As winter approached, his workload increased and there were numerous late meetings and business dinners. The frost on the air sharpened the senses and his guilt blew in through the front door with a gust on the evening chill.

Once or twice I sniffed his discarded shirt before stuffing it into the laundry basket. He must have seen me do this. The familiar perfume soon disappeared from his clothes. I experienced a brief moment of joy that I had never challenged him on his infidelity, but the smell on his Jermyn Street pure Egyptian cotton was soon replaced with the musky odour of passion. And it wasn't ours.

Not only did I know things had gone too far, I knew he was actively controlling his deceit.

*

96

They say the best cuisine is prepared on a gas stove. For obvious reasons it's not safe for me to cook over a live flame. Induction hobs, with their ability to instantly heat and cool, perfectly mirror the precision of gas. A Dutch appliance company has adapted theirs for people like me, fitting surfaces with an extra contrast silicone coating, allowing the sensitive hands of the sightless to master the most delicate of recipes.

With my developed cooking skills, the stove has become an extension of my body. I know where all the buttons and slides are. I don't need a timer, the one in my brain is as good an indication as any clock, aided by taste, smell and touch.

He will be late again tonight. Tuesday has become their regular night. Occasionally he says he won't be home for dinner at all. But when I asked him this morning whether he would be here for a meal, I detected a hint of guilt when he said he'd be late. He'd hesitated, then said yes, he would be back for dinner. He said I should start without him and to put his in the warming drawer.

Jake wants his cake and he wants to eat it too.

I prepare an aromatic paste of coriander, cumin, marjoram, and harissa. I crush the dried spices with the mortar and pestle and mix in the chilli sauce. The spice stings my nostrils, and tears spring to my sightless eyes.

Italian extra virgin olive with a high acidity is my oil of choice. It thins as it warms and I feel the tiny weight of it slithering around as I gently tip the pan from side to side. I heat it just enough so it doesn't smoke, catching the pungent scent before it goes too far. The perfect aroma of a Calabrian summer's evening tells me when it's ready to receive the meat.

At the back of the fridge is a pair of chicken breasts, forgotten for a number of weeks. I had meant to throw the meat out, but it has avoided my searching hands on the shelf. I mark packages of food on each level with pieces of electrical tape or rubber bands, depending on their contents and when they've been purchased. The one I found this afternoon is well past its use-by date.

I slather the chicken in the sauce to mask the gangrenous smell that hits me when I tear off the plastic packaging. I slip it into the hot oil, and the gagging stench is sucked up the steam extractor, replaced by my careful balance of gourmet spices. I use my finger to judge the elasticity, the meat only just warmed through, the tell-tale raw juices running together with chilli. Tonight I will tell him I've already eaten. Anyway my hunger has long been quashed.

Perched on a plate of aromatic rice and finely chopped vegetables, I slide the chicken dish onto the table as I hear his key in the door. I put on my best smile.

Revenge is best served half-cooked.

Lipstick
by Amy Macrae

Shortlisted, Edinburgh Award for Flash Fiction 2022

'You look beautiful,' she says, smiling at me in the mirror. Her eyes flicker to meet mine before she blends and buffs the last touches of powder into my cheeks.

'Spice it up' is printed in tiny lettering on the base of the lipstick. I grip the shimmering tube tightly, as if it might disappear any moment.

I walk along Multree Walk, a warm glow filling my insides, making my peach cheeks flush pink. I count my breaths. I feel the rhythm of my life slow, my chest loosen and the pain of living lighten a little on my shoulders.

As I open the door to the flat, I smell his aftershave and my stomach knots. A sea of snakes slither in the shallow water of my stomach. I hear the drop of heavy feet on the carpet and pounding steps getting closer. I keep my hands pressed to the cool door, trying to find those long breaths. Those long, languid breaths of a person who felt happy, unburdened but they were buried deep, now submerged in the water as dread thrashes around the pit of my stomach.

I turn. He laughs. A hearty laugh, long and theatrical that fills the small hallway as I make myself smaller.

'You look ridiculous,' he says.

I'm still holding the lipstick I realise. So tightly that the plastic is pressing ridges into my skin. He grabs my hand and squeezes until it falls. I fall and the tears begin falling too.

Spaceship Head
by Karen Storey

Longlisted, Scottish Arts Club Short Story Competition 2022

There she is, creeping out of the house, glancing in my direction. Too late, Spaceship Head, it's me, Bethany, your delightful neighbour, just across the way.

Yes, it's a funny nickname, isn't it? You watch, she'll pretend she doesn't see us standing on my doorstep. Hear that noise? The black bin liner clinks its Sunday morning tune of empty glass bottles as she makes her way towards her grey rubbish bin. What's your guess? Seven bottles this week, thirteen? Naughty of her not to put those bottles in her red recycling box. But I know why she won't bring that red plastic box out of her garage.

Anyway, this is my car here, the silver Vauxhall. Is this a new scratch on my door? No, it must be an old one. Spaceship wouldn't dare go that far.

Before we get in the car, let's wait, see if she looks across. Perhaps for the first time in months, she'll acknowledge me. Watch, she's lifting the lid of her grey wheelie bin, her bicep rising in that sinewy arm. She works out, you know, a lot. Sometimes even right there on her front lawn, showing off her broomstick body in pink day-glo leggings and vest, Arctic Monkeys blasting out of her Bluetooth speaker, dumb-bells spread on the grass. She's nuts.

Crash! She's dropped the bag in the bin. Now she's turning towards us, but oh, with a face as red as her house's brickwork, and just as rough. Watch as her gaze skims past me, past you, and now it rests slightly to our right. Bravo, great performance, Spaceship Head. I'm still invisible.

Oh, sorry, did I not explain why she's called Spaceship Head? My sister made it up months back. We saw her outside her house with this new hair style. She'd dyed it silver like that character from *Frozen*. It had also been cut into a short bob but was styled so wide, my sister said her head looked like one those flying saucers we'd seen in cartoons as kids. We stumbled into my house laughing. She's been Spaceship Head to us since. My sister knows, you see, how I've tried to create harmony between Spaceship Head and me these last few months.

Twice, I've left home-made salted caramel brownies on her doorstep knowing they're her favourite. Each time, she came out, read the note on the box, then stomped over it before dumping the cardboard mess into the bin. Last March, I bought a young cherry blossom tree and left that for her too. It was only about four-feet-tall. She'd told me once she had a corner space in her garden crying out for something pretty. I really thought she'd like it. Instead, she broke that young tree in pieces, my own heart splintering with every branch she deliberately snapped. She then shoved the murdered tree into her green garden recycling bin.

Come on, let's stop talking about this. We're on our way to do something wholesome. That yoga class starts in twenty minutes. It'll be good to chill out, breathe in pure intentions, golden light. As we breathe out, we can send her healing vibes. What did you say? I'm a nice person? Forgiving? Well, it's a decision to emit positivity or poison towards others.

Wait. I'll tell you something else about Spaceship Head. She stole that red recycling box. It's mine. Bit of a cheek, right? Especially when she just keeps it in her garage. I went out one Monday morning after the bin men came. I looked across the street and two red boxes were outside her house. The bin men must have thrown mine over to her side. I stepped across the road to retrieve it but she rushed out, grabbed both boxes and ran inside.

I shouted, 'That's mine!'

She slammed her front door. I told you, she's nuts. The next Monday morning I watched her scamper out carrying the red box of bottles, packed so tightly they didn't so much clink but lightly chime. When she strode back indoors, I rushed across, picked up the red box, then dumped her numerous empty wine bottles into her grey bin. I brought the box home.

Later, while I was out, she came across and told my boyfriend I stole her box. He believed her, the idiot, and gave it back. James and I had a big row over that. Afterward I decided not to allow Spaceship to cause any more disharmony in my home. I silently forgave her and let her keep that ridiculous box as it meant so much to her.

Let's get to that yoga class. Oh look, here's James, coming back from his jog. He's lovely, isn't he? We've got a moment, say hello. God, look at him standing there in the middle of the road gazing at her house. He's probably wondering if she still has that red recycling box. Oh good, he's seen us, he's waving. Put down your window, I'll lean across to shout out.

'Darling, I'm just off to yoga with my new friend. I'll see you in a while. I'll be back before lunch.'

Look at that smile, those gorgeous grey eyes. You must come back for coffee after class, meet him properly. Right, let's get off to the village hall and get our mats down. I don't want to get stuck at the back like last week.

One more thing. Spaceship Head and I were once friends. No, really. We'd sit in my garden on a Sunday afternoon drinking herbal tea. One afternoon, this time last year, she sent a text saying her husband's playing golf and did I want to come over to hers for tea and sunbathing? I said yes, changed into my black bikini, wrapped on a matching sarong. On my way out, I thought to hell with tea, it's a hot, sunny day. I went into the kitchen and pulled an ice-cold bottle of Sauvignon plonk from the fridge. When I arrived on her doorstep with the bottle, I swear underneath her suntan her face went white.

'No,' she said, 'I don't drink.'

'Oh. Not even one glass?'

Her eyes softened and with a sad smile she shook her head. She then dropped her smile and said 'Okay. Just one.'

I followed her down the hallway into her spotless kitchen. She pulled a white wooden chair towards one of her cupboards to reach a shelf high up, pushing aside some blue ceramic cups to retrieve two wine glasses.

We sat in the garden chatting about her physio work and my job at the vintage clothing boutique in town, laughing at our stories of strange customers. She kept pulling up the straps of her brown bikini top, why I'm not sure. You've seen her, she's skinny with boobs like wet teabags, hardly big enough to need support. Anyway, within half an hour she drunk most of that bottle. She actually turned it upside down to shake the last drops of the wine into her glass then asked if I had another bottle I could go and grab. Perhaps her brain had already embarked on its own spaceship mission.

We heard her front door slam, her husband coming in from golf. Suddenly, she threw the empty bottle into the lilac bush then picked up our two wine glasses, tossing those into the shrub roses behind. I wouldn't have minded but my glass was still half full. Her face was flushed as he stepped out on to the grass but she put on a tight grin and offered him a cup of tea. He walked to the side of the garden, pulled over a lawn chair and sat down opposite us. With a relaxed smile, he told her he'd love a cuppa.

Spaceship Head went inside. I felt self-conscious, aware I was sitting there in a skimpy black bikini in front of James. Yes, I said James. I already told you he was there. Aren't you listening? Oh wait. I don't think I explained this part. James is Spaceship's husband. Anyway, he asked me politely about my work at the boutique, while his eyes travelled over me, lingering on the scant black triangles of my bikini top. Yes, he's her husband. They're still married, but he lives with me now. Anyway, I'm trying to explain. He asked how I enjoyed living in the neighbourhood. I said fine, I'd been in my house for a year and felt at home, apart from the problem with my conservatory door. He said it wasn't good for a woman living on her own to have a faulty lock.

Late that evening he knocked on my door with his bag of tools.

103

It was warm.

I was wearing shorts.

He was kind.

Within minutes he'd fixed that lock. I offered him a drink and poured us some Hennessy. We sat down on my two-seater sofa and he complimented me on my taste in Cognac, while staring at my bare legs. He asked why a woman like me lived alone. I explained about the divorce, how my ex was a narcissist. I told James how some narcissists project their condition onto their partners instead of accepting the problem was them. My marriage had been doomed from the start.

James was sympathetic. He put his hand on my bare thigh claiming I deserved better.

Yes, yes. It started then.

Why are you looking at me like that? Okay, I know what you're about to say. You're thinking about that recycling box, aren't you? That stealing it is her retribution. As if a stupid plastic box could take the place of a man like James. Let me guess, you also think stomping on brownies and murdering that defenceless tree is also her revenge. I bet you assume she scratched my car. But you're wrong. Her retaliation is more calculated. You don't think I've stood at her door a dozen times when it first happened, stooping, stuttering, begging forgiveness? Pleading I'd never meant harm but that once we'd started we couldn't stop? Explained the gut-curdling nausea I feel whenever I step outside my house and look across to hers? She keeps up this feud to punish, to play and taunt. Yes, I'm sure she's hurting but she knows this guilt is chilling my soul, turning it to ice then slowly snapping it into sharp pieces like the cherry tree she killed.

She won't move house. What? I should move? No. I want to fix this. I've spent months being kind. Nothing works. Wait, maybe that's it. Forget yoga. I have an idea. I'm stopping the car. Let's pick up all those red boxes outside these other houses. As many as we can get. Let's dump them all on Spaceship's lawn. No, listen.

Kindness isn't working, this is a better plan. Make her angry. Enough to break through her rough red-brick wall of hatred. I'll break her like she broke that young tree. Break her until the emotional sap weeps out of her and she has no other choice but to seep her forgiveness on to me.

Come on, get out. Help me get these boxes.

What do you mean, 'No'? I'll pull over here, just out of sight.

Wait. Look in your wing mirror. That's James crossing the road back there. Oh my God. He's letting himself into Spaceship's house. He still has a key?

No.

James, what are you doing?

That's Spaceship's hand on his shoulder guiding him in.

Breathe. I'm just paranoid. He would never choose her over me. He probably wants to smooth the feud.

What did you say? I'd deserve it if he went back?

Right, put your seatbelt back on. We're going. There's a road towards the motorway just here.

It doesn't matter where. The question is how long it takes for me to explain, for you to understand and to stop your judgemental thoughts. I've got hours.

And hours.

Until you see.

The Bench
by Lynsey Clark

Longlisted, Scottish Arts Club Short Story Competition 2022

Anna sat on the bench; her eyes closed. Around her, birds chirped noisily in conversation, their voices amplified in the open space of the park. She listened intently to the changing tones of the twitters.

It was one of those strange days in early May — frequently moving clouds ensuring that fleeting moments of sunshine were quickly replaced by cold winds and showers. The uncertainty of it had thankfully guaranteed that the normally busy park was almost deserted.

Sensing movement, she turned to see a familiar figure sitting down beside her; an elderly man she'd seen in the park many times from a distance. He had a face full of character, well-established deep lines carved into his forehead and wild eyebrows with their own rules of direction. Wisps of white hair escaped from his tweed trilby hat. A small, scruffy black terrier settled into a resting position at his feet.

Anna smiled and returned her gaze forward. The art of conversation had abandoned her recently.

'Strange day isn't it,' he said.

His voice was almost as she expected — deep and gravelly — but his accent was hard to place. Scottish, but it didn't sound local to Lanarkshire. He suited being old, she thought; she couldn't imagine that he'd ever looked any different.

'It is,' she replied. 'I'm glad I've got my jacket now, but it was so lovely earlier.'

'Ah yes, things can change in a hurry,' he nodded. She looked round. *Things do change in a hurry.*

They had a Christmas shopping day planned. Her mum was looking after the children so they could enjoy a day out, just the two of them. They talked about it for days leading up to it, such was the rarity of a child-free trip. But it was such a gorgeous morning, Tommy decided to take the bike out for a *quick spin* before they left.

'It's a cracking day for it — I'll be back in an hour,' he had promised.

'The birds are making themselves heard today,' the old man continued. 'See the swallows have finally arrived. Hardy wee buggers, I always admire them.'

Anna looked up at the row of white chested birds perched on a wire above. 'I've never paid much attention to them.'

'Imagine those wee things flying all the way to Africa and back,' he nodded towards them.

'I wish I had their energy,' Anna said. The sun had momentarily broken through the clouds, forcing her to screw up her eyes.

The woman in the car behind said the sun was blinding. There's no way he would have seen the corner. The young police officer had stood in Anna's hall, her eyes glancing awkwardly to the family photographs on the wall as she spoke. Anna was only half listening. She'd known as soon as she heard the knock at the door.

'You have plenty energy,' said the man.

'Sorry?'

'I've seen you with your wee ones,' he continued. 'Running around after them. Takes some chasing, that boy of yours.'

Anna laughed. 'Yeah, he's fast. He loves running. Not so keen on schoolwork.'

'Ah, it's not for everyone.'

She smiled. 'He is happy when he's running.'

107

She had almost stopped herself before the words came out, hoping to preserve their innocence as long as possible. *How can he be dead? He's only 40 and Grandpa's 72 and he's not even dead!* They cried themselves to sleep, then the next morning, asked if Daddy was home yet. This went on for weeks before they finally accepted, he really wasn't coming home. That was somehow worse.

'You'll not need to buy tomato sauce anymore,' Ellie had announced in her matter-of-fact tone one day, peering in the open kitchen cupboard. 'Dad was the only one that liked it.'

'Your wee girl – she's like you, isn't she?' he said.

She wondered if he paid this much attention to everyone he saw in the park. 'Do you think? I don't really see it.'

'She was having a cuddle with Jess here the other day. Has a way with animals, I'd say.'

'Yeah, she does. She loves them.' Anna closed her eyes in an effort to stem the tears.

The puppy had been due to be picked up the week before Christmas. It was something they'd talked about for years, but now the children were a bit older, it seemed like the right time. She was the smallest one in the litter. White, mainly, with little dots of black on each leg. They'd argued over names on the way home. 'Lightening!'. 'No actually, Thunderstorm!', this from Jake.

'Maybe something shorter, buddy, punchier? Mind we're going to be shouting its name across the park,' Tommy suggested, glancing at Anna.

'Why do we need to wait a whole 42 days? I'm going to score the days off on my calendar,' Ellie proclaimed. She had only got two days marked off before their lives changed forever.

'We were going to get a dog, last year,' Anna found herself saying.

'Dot. We were going to call her Dot.'

The lady had been very understanding. 'Don't worry, it's completely fine, in the circumstances. We've had lots of enquiries, so we'll find her a new home in no time.'

She couldn't bear the extra responsibility. She kept thinking of its expectant little face, looking up at her, trusting her. She already had two children doing the same.

'Dot's a good name. Was my wife's,' he said.

'Really? Is she no longer with you?'

'No, no, passed away a few years ago now.'

'Sorry to hear that.'

'Aye. Just me and this wee scruff now.' The little dog wagged its tail in acknowledgement. 'She's good company though,' he paused. 'We think we're looking after them, but it's the other way round really.'

The wind picked up again. They pulled their coats tighter as they sat in companionable silence, neither of them in a hurry to go anywhere. Anna watched the dog, contentedly huddled into its old chum. She wondered if she'd ever feel contentment again. Yet Tommy used to joke, 'You'd find hope in a hopeless situation.'

'Life's simple for the animals,' the old man said, as if reading her mind. 'If they lose their mate, they find a new one. We've complicated things, us humans. Became too clever for our own good.'

'Yeah,' she nodded. 'You're probably right.'

Jake and Ellie hadn't seemed surprised when she told them they could no longer get the pup, like they were already resigned to the fact that nothing good would ever happen in their lives again.

'It's fine, Mum. It was Dad that really wanted a dog anyway,' Jake said, the two of them sloping off to their rooms. But when she thought of their early excitement and Ellie crossing off the days with her different coloured glitter pens, it caused a tightening in her chest that almost halted her breath.

109

'I sometimes think though, is it really worth it?' she spoke her thoughts aloud. The old man looked at her curiously.

'Like, I really wanted children. We both did,' she continued. 'But as soon as they're born, you have this love for them that's almost painful. The thought of anything happening to them is so unbearable, it hurts just thinking about it. Why do we do it to ourselves?'

He laughed. 'Well, I suppose, if you want the highs, you need to accept the lows. That's just the way of it.'

'Would you really want to go through life with none of those highs; those moments of pure joy?' he added. 'Is travelling on a long, straight road, with big hedges on each side, more attractive than one with hills and bends and beautiful scenery?'

Anna had been admiring the view from the top of Ben Lomond when she first met Tommy. She was on a hen weekend at Loch Lomond and he was there with some friends. The two groups got talking at the top of the mountain. He told her later that night that watching her looking at the view, was better than the view itself.

'Do you use that line every time you climb a mountain?' she asked sceptically.

'First one I've scaled, to be honest,' he had replied. 'But if it works, I'll keep it in mind for my next hike. There's bound to be countless big hills in Scotland with gorgeous girls waiting at the top,' he winked.

The choir of tweets restarted from the power line above and Anna looked up to see the row of swallows had multiplied in numbers. Brightness was breaking through the clouds and she felt the fog in her head clearing slightly.

'You wondering what's making that noise, Jess, eh?' the old man asked. The dog looked up suspiciously, one ear cocked in consideration.

'How did you manage to find those moments of joy again though, after you lost your wife?' she asked.

The old man considered the question. 'It wasn't easy,' he replied eventually. 'There were times I wished I could have gone with her. Wondered what the point was. But every stage of life has its challenges. I suppose you either face them and try to beat them; or give up.' He reached down and patted the wee dog. She rubbed against him appreciatively.

'There's a lot of skill involved in being happy, you know. It doesn't just happen – you need to work at it.'

The bike had been Tommy's 40th birthday present to himself. His friends joked it was a mid-life crisis. 'You'll need to watch him now, Anna. Next thing he'll be speeding into the sunset with a 22-year-old biker chick, fully clad in leather.' Anna went along with the joke, but she didn't really mind. She knew he had always wanted one.

'I've found one!' he came home, delighted with himself one day. 'It's a Triumph Bonneville. A classic! Needs a bit of work on it, so I can get it at a good price,' he beamed.

'Right, smashing'. Anna rolled her eyes.

She touched her wet cheeks, the tears streaming steadily now. He didn't acknowledge that she was crying or ask her why, but it didn't feel uncomfortable. She hadn't cried much in the last six months, in an effort to be strong for the children. A blanket of sadness had been draped over the three of them and they'd carried it around with its accumulating weight. Allowing the tears to come seemed to lift it slightly.

'But how can you be happy when part of you is missing?' she said.

'You find a different kind of happiness,' he replied.

They had spent a lot of time outdoors last May, when the weather was warm and dry for a few weeks in succession. The two of them lay in the garden, while the children played in the tent they'd been sleeping in for several nights. 'This is what it's all about,' Tommy said.

'Lying in the sun doing nothing,' she laughed. 'While the house is an absolute riot.'

'Lying in the sun, appreciating what we've got,' he answered. 'Listening to the kids chatting away. This is all we need.' They lay with their eyes closed, feeling the warmth from the sun and each other.

'You know what would make it even better?' he nudged her. 'Go get me a beer out the fridge.'

'Go get it yourself,' she had pushed him off the blanket. 'I'm enjoying the moment.'

The sun was on their faces now in the park. Anna glanced at her watch, 2.40pm. 'I can't believe that's the time, I better go.' She got up, reluctantly. 'It was lovely to meet you. I'm sure I'll see you here another day.'

'Aye. I'll maybe meet you out walking a wee dog of your own someday,' he winked.

'Maybe,' she smiled, turning to lift her bag from the bench. The sun glinted off a brass plaque fixed on the wood that she hadn't noticed before. *Dot's Bench* it read.

'Is that...?' she turned to ask.

But he was gone.

The lonely man
by Tim Roelandt

Shortlisted, Edinburgh Award for Flash Fiction 2022

David took the same path from work daily. Even blindfolded, he would have known where to step, pivot, or sway to reach the front door of his one-room apartment physically unscathed. Every evening, David would pass by the old man sitting on the park bench with his cane resting between his corduroy-covered knees, his gaze fixated upon the surface of the pond as it refracted the autumn sunlight. David often wondered about this codger. He would imagine him living in some dilapidated house, forgotten by an indifferent world, with nothing to live for except his solemn routines. Thinking about this made David's chest and throat feel constricted as if squeezed by an invisible hand. This old man conjured up in David a profound melancholy.

One day, instead of walking by, as usual, David joined the old man on the bench — his motive unclear. The old man greeted David's polite nod with a kind smile. As David was struggling to produce something pleasantly banal to say, the old man initiated:

'I see you walk by every day, young man.' He looked forward with his hands folded atop his cane.

'Forgive my candor,' — his eyes now met David's — 'but you have the gait of someone going down a lonesome road. If you want to talk...'

Sudden and copious were the tears that trickled down David's face. Sorrow was the only response he could muster.

'That's okay,' said the man, gently patting David's knee. 'We can just sit here awhile, together.'

A Love Letter
by Sarah Brown

Longlisted, Scottish Arts Club Short Story Competition 2022

My friends always talked about you. After university, they were all riding that motorway, heading straight to your bright lights and bold promises. The names beat loudly. 'Where are you living?' They wanted to know how to navigate someone as complicated, as enigmatic as you. You're the big smoke — an environmental and emotional storm. A flat in Putney. A loft in Bermondsey. A house share in Highbury. Those parts of you were like keys to your doors; everyone wanted to show that they knew you best, all your secret staircases and hidden west wings.

You entertained them for a while. They went on Spare Room and Hinge, hung up fairy lights and polaroids, posed for a little while in 'content creating' or 'social curating' and sold their souls to futures in finance. But people would sacrifice those things for you, on the altar of your myths.

Over catch-ups, I found out more about your charm. One friend was dancing through rainbows of 40s nostalgia in the West End. The other was working in a CBD shop with an investment banker boyfriend who traded shares in Bitcoin at the weekend. A third wrote children's books and was building an app that would 'streamline' something. Don't ask me what. The same words bounced on pogo sticks of youth, popping kernels of adventure into cinematic dreams. 'So fun!' 'Great vibe!' 'Fast pace.' 'Living my best life.'

Life could only be the best with you. Apparently.

From a stratosphere of superlatives, I began to sketch you — the romantic, the player, the alpha-male. A real keeper.

But these lovers of yours were realistic too. They'd say they needed a break from you. You were 'a lot.' I started to crave you — I wanted to be with someone who could be so much, so fast, so all at once that I might just need a break from them too.

I made applications furiously. Anyone, anything that could give me an introduction to you. It didn't need to be right up my street.

With a deep gulp of breath, I confessed — what you wanted to hear. I knew your 'type', the kinds of things that turned you on. I would work hard (I could get to love shares and contract prices and closing deals and posturing and diets of Pret and 'kind regards' and empty 'hope you're well's', of course I could!). I could be that cool, flared jean-wearing, kombucha-drinking, podcast-making kind of independent. A go-getter. A grafter. Type 'A' personality.

Somewhere inside of me, you had already whispered, 'Prove it.'

But I did.

And when I met you off the train at Clapham Junction that first morning, you smiled, briefly. You knew what was coming. It happened in lightning strikes. Warning letters flashed across the screen. STAND BACK. STAND BACK. Why? I barely had time to ask. Tunnels of dark thundered. Louder, louder, louder. Now! The great, big, ugly bustle of your red, white and blue blew me away, pulled me closer, hugged me tightly, kissed me with phones, delays, people, poverty, wealth, stories.

You boomed from your arms and into my heart. It couldn't have been any more dramatic.

We made love a lot those first few months. It was that kind of frenetic love that's keen to please. Gliding through the Serpentine, the galleries, lying on the grass at the V&A, inhaling Dior and Japan and the Classics, drawing me out for strolls in the evening through Kensington High Street – it was an endless honeymoon.

In August, you dressed up for our dates. I saw you at your best. You exhaled the heat of the day, cooling it with your breath, and opened your eyes to kiss me amidst the balmy, twilight glades of Hyde Park.

You led a busy life — I couldn't just depend on you. You taught me how to keep on top of friendships; places I could study quietly in the mornings; where to find romantic bookshops; the kinds of coats that would keep clean while I explored the veins of your great, throbbing centre.

You giggled when I stood in the middle of the escalator. You whispered, teasingly, 'Keep right.'

Do you remember the Hampstead days? The mountainous explorations? When we climbed those red brick avenues, panted, paused, went for brunch, posed about, bought an overpriced punnet of raspberries and walked for miles? As if by walking all that way I could, somehow, know you, be with you, hold you, possess you. But you are full of false summits.

The closest I got was Parliament Hill. We were above your cranes, your skyscrapers, your high rises, your insatiable efforts to be seen. That's where you get your kicks — being seen.

I saw you. I saw your pastel villas that beamed like humongous dolls-houses in Primrose Hill. The sugar blue sky suited you. You liked the attention. Why shouldn't I look inside?

'Let's walk on.' You smiled. We didn't want to get to the park too late. But it wasn't too late.

I did a double-take. And all those things I didn't know about you clung to me, deftly, sharply. Two corpses in sleeping bags. One coughed through a face twisted somewhere between chaos and laughter.

Suddenly, a tall women emerged from a lime green palace. She held a Portuguese Water Dog in front of her, Charlie, on its way to 'Pooches & Smooches' every Thursday (which was today), after Matilde, the housekeeper had taken him for a morning walk before she returned to prepare a dairy-free, sugar-free sweet potato gratin for Maisy and Sophia who were to be picked up at 5:30pm today and not 6:30pm because French with Monsieur LeCliffe was cancelled this week which is disappointing really because Monsieur LeCliffe had been told (yes, he had been told) that the girls would be going to Aix-en-Provence in two weeks' time for half-term.

I felt sick.

You didn't understand.

'Why does it matter?' you asked me. 'The world isn't fair, what's the point in being so judgmental?'

'Judgemental!' I screamed at you. 'Why did you keep secrets from me? How could you lead me on?'

You didn't say anything back. What did I expect?

At the gates of Regent's Park, the sun started setting over February. It was not quite winter, not quite spring. I began to walk. Your chill, silent air slid down my collar, down my spine.

*

Soon my body got tired with making love to you. We got a change of scene. We went south. We poured along the Southbank, saw plays at the National, time travelled back to your grand fairs and exhibitions. You opened up to me between endless sky and sweeps of green and bursts of colour. You made me laugh and cry at the monkey puzzle of your past in Kew and Richmond. I really wanted to make it work.

And for a while, it did. I was strict. At 6am I filled my lungs with the oxygen of all that was good about you. Yoga. Run. At 7am, I showered in water that tasted like rotten eggs and stained the steel with limescale. At 8am I began the journey to your core, greedy with an assortment of frowns, elbows and armpits of Lynx, pulsating with your gigantic heartbeats too.

I didn't look for your scabs. I didn't want to pick on you. But after a while, the wounds were weeping uncontrollably.

Couldn't I fix you? When the thunder stopped and the tunnel ended, we hit a dead end. There was something rotten inside you.

I blew your soot from my nostrils. You frowned at me on the escalator: 'I might not be as happy as some, but I am richer.'

117

I looked. In semicircle windows you advertised Rolexes with Daniel Craig as your dependably English cover boy. In streets that cut through equality like a needle and thread, your tight-suited, navy disciples worshipped you till 3am.

And you rewarded them. Sushi-places, fabulous sky-bars. But I couldn't help thinking, 'Don't you shit it all out, just the same?'

It never failed to amaze me, that animation with which carnivorous lovers talked about you. Despite all your excess and waste (or perhaps because of it) you still turned them on. These lovers could settle for cupboards at £1,000 a month. They were 'living their best life'. Apparently.

But who hadn't strolled by your slumped hunches, the darker parts of you, those who numbed themselves from a consciousness that would kill them, those who tossed between a thrill through the arm or a leap into the Thames? That was their daily commute. Their best life.

Sometimes, while you slept and I stared at a ceiling, I saw your eyes twitch a little with the things you'd left behind. I heard the howls. Did they wake you? In those twitches, your ghosts crowded together and tried to burst through the gates of your steely gleam. I heard that nightmarish siege try to grip you into destroying the shards and gherkins and cheese-graters and walky-talkies and other ridiculously still-life named buildings that bellowed one single reverence –

MONEY.

They didn't wake you, those lonely, lost exes of yours. The thud of the last tube blew a foghorn through their resistance. Louder, louder, louder — silence.

The parts of me that had sparkled with love for you at Clapham were nothing now but bits of sandpaper. The gentleness would weaken me, the uncertainties would roughen me. All that was left were cobwebs mourning a life that had long moved out. I was smoothed with complicity.

And yet, the sandpaper scratched. Your whining voice couldn't understand the way I said my name. You dragged me to 'cool' restaurants and made me pay for avocados that were browned or coffee that was never just coffee. It was never easy to find you, to love you, to hold you.

I began to doubt if you had any real inside. You were all inside out.

You told me people would die for you. As if you saw my ugliness, you hesitated, 'Do you need a moment?' God, I needed a lifetime.

I left you.

The world shut down at 4pm. I rang out the emotions, drunken and tired from the body they had beaten down. I sat in the bath and ripped my skin till I bled. I ripped up the skin that had walked till I held you. The skin that had thought you could love me back.

*

I've noticed people like to say things. 'Practice makes perfect.' 'Things take time.' 'Just be patient.' 'Hard work always pays off.' True. But what about the things we already possess?

You never took your medicine in the end. I took mine — self-acceptance. I've learned a lot about pride. I've learned that it stings, implodes on itself like a suicidal chemical reaction to push and push and push. The poison fills your head. Louder, louder, louder.

Until we accept — you can't help the way you are. People have fled to you, flourished and flowered with you. You don't just wine and dine the Eton messes; you shelter the adventurers who mould you with their views.

But, as for me, I've climbed the mountain, got to the top and decided that I don't like the view. I've come back down. And doesn't everyone, in the end?

My eyes close and I'm on Parliament Hill with you. But I'm really looking out this time. The towers and turrets and tips are showing me something else. I can see how I got here; I can see why I wanted you. But don't get me wrong. There're other chapters. Plenty of fish and all that.

So, London, baby, let's stay friends. Let's keep in touch. You taught me so much. I kept right, eventually. Except, now, it's more like keeping right by me.

Green Dreams
by Edith Reznák

Commendation, Edinburgh Award for Flash Fiction 2022

It all started on the 7:15 IC train towards Budapest. *The Great Gatsby* lay open in my lap and I glanced up to see *Tender Is the Night* under your arm, a perfect coincidence.

'Boats against the current?' you asked and I smiled because your eyes were the exact shade of green I'd always imagined for the light at the end of Daisy's dock. You dropped into the empty seat next to mine and we talked all the way to the station. I was supposed to attend Aunt Mari's card game, but you bought me a glass of mulled wine as we strolled along the River Danube to watch the city lights flicker to life. But the one you lit in my heart shone so bright, nothing, not even the endless winter days could put it out when I learned you only read Fitzgerald because a professor assigned it, threw your dirty clothes all over the place, and I was more like my mother than I wished to admit.

'What if we're just not meant to be?' I asked once, leaning against the locked bathroom door, wiping my tears away.

'Then we'll just stretch our arms farther, until —'

A whistle blew, the daydream shattered, but you finally looked up, locking your gaze with mine. 'We'll make it?' I mouthed just when my train lurched forward and yours rushed the opposite direction, its green taillamp slipping further and further away until the darkness swallowed it.

Stella
by Jessica Redfern

Longlisted, Scottish Arts Club Short Story Competition 2022

Stella was old, ancient. She croaked when she talked like a rusty old engine. Grey hair came in wisps down a long neck, skin loose and shrivelled, marked and spotted. Eyes small and blue, knowing and sharp. I wondered how it must feel to wake up in that skin. In that wrinkled skin. What it would feel like to live amongst your things, faded, chipped and musty. Decades worth of memories. How must it feel to walk a little less every day? To see a little less, to breathe a little less easy. To know that time is creeping up, waiting, standing just behind you. To know that soon there will be no teapots or saucepans, no biscuit tins or tablecloths. All these things, the useful ones and the treasures, the photographs and the memories, soon to be dispersed and lost, broken and gone. Whether she thought about it I could not say, for a fire still burned in Stella, a spirit so bright it was as young as a bud on an apple tree. Her spirit blew around this place like a westerly wind.

Stella was my neighbour. She was alone or I might have hidden away from her. I like my own company and I feel disturbed by the spirit of others. Spirits are forceful, demanding, I don't like to be in their way. But somehow, slowly, over the garden fence, something had formed. On her side, the garden was full of flowers and random objects; a rusty old anvil, a coal scuttle full of rainwater, the grate of a Victorian fireplace. On my side, mainly concrete and engine parts, plastic tubs that used to have flowers in before Jade left me.

Stella liked to talk, she talked about lots of things; about rabbits she'd kept as a child, about villages in Spain, about her late husband who had also liked engines and he'd fixed lawnmowers for people from the town. She talked about her niece in Scotland, caravans in Wales, her father who had smoked thin cigarettes and made his own ale.

She grew things, potatoes, leeks, beans. She liked to garden. In the summer she would be out in a polyester dress, loose skin hanging from bare arms. I wondered how it felt, her body fading like the daffodils on her compost heap.

On Saturdays I went round for tea. I can't remember when it started, and sometimes I worried how I would get out of it if something came up, like a girlfriend or a job. The routine had become so fixed that everything in my week rolled around it and I was always there at half past one. The tea was in the teapot, the cups waiting, the milk was in a metal jug. Stella had chosen one of her charity-shop mugs to be mine. It had a cartoon on it of a man in a flatcap. She made the same cakes every week, small sponge ones in paper cases. There was always a meat pie and bread and butter. Sometimes I ate it, sometimes the smell of meat, of old carpets, of old Stella filled my nostrils and I didn't care for it. Sometimes, though I did. She talked and talked about her brother Harold, about his farm in Scotland, about her father's pigeons, about her friend from church who was losing her hair. She talked and she knitted. As far as I knew all the jumpers she knitted came to me. I had about two a year, passed over the fence. I wore them just to please her when I was outside fixing the bikes.

Then one day everything changed. For a start it was a Tuesday, not a Saturday. I was tatting with an old motorbike out the back when I looked up to find those shrivelled blue eyes on me. Stella was at the fence. I waited for that croaky voice.

'Have you ever grown carrots, Matthew?'

The question was innocent enough, but as always with Stella, I felt like I was being pulled into a tide. Something sad and powerful was filling the air around her. I wanted no part in it.

'I've never grown nothing.' I looked down at the engine at my feet, I don't grow things I thought, I take them apart.

She came closer, leaned over the fence with those baggy arms. I waited for one of her stories. I waited for her to take me with her to her dad's allotment, her brother's farm, the backstreet terraces where she'd grown up.

'Hop over this fence, I need your help,' was all she said.

'My help?'

'My back's not what it was, lad. I'm getting old you know.'

'You could have fooled me.'

There was a twinkle in those steely eyes. We both knew she was as fit as ten men, but then again, her back did seem more hunched these days. She was starting to curl up like a hedgehog in a ball. I shrugged and put the spanner down and I climbed over the fence.

*

'Hold out your hand.' She was holding an envelope that had come from the council, out of it and into my hand she shook a pile of tiny brown husks. 'Carrot seeds,' she said. 'Collected them from last year.'

I looked down at the little specks, hardly seeds at all, more like bits of grain that might blow away any second.

'The grounds warming up now,' she said. 'It's time.'

She showed me where to plant them in the soil that was ready, in rows or drills as she called them. It made me think of them as little soldiers standing in line. She talked about the soil, how it couldn't be too rich or they wouldn't grow downwards, she talked about carrot-fly and companion plants. There wasn't much that Stella didn't know about carrots.

Afterwards she made tea in the pot and brought it out. Brought out my mug and the biscuit tin. She only ever had Rich Tea biscuits. Always only Rich Tea biscuits in this tin and boiled sweets in another tin. I wondered as I dipped two into my tea, whether she ever felt like a change, was ever tempted by all the others in the shop.

124

There didn't seem much wrong with her back now as she squatted down on the grass to drink her tea. We watched the ants climbing up the old apple tree and she told me about her Dad's sweetpeas, 'Sweetpeas need a long root growth. We'll plant them in toilet rolls.'

Almost every day after that, she would coax me over the fence until I just started getting up and going. Once again I was swept away by the power of her spirit. It was as wide as the summer sky, as industrious as the bees on the lavender, as powerful as the force that was swelling the trees. We planted potatoes, beetroot and broccoli. We planted sweetpeas and beans, tomatoes and lettuce. We planted and we watched. We watched the carrot shoots push up through the ground, we watched the buds turn to apples on the old tree and we watched the ants going up and down. And I listened. I listened to stories of pears and damsons, of jam and blackberries. I listened about compost, about worms, about maybugs and ladybirds, about mint and rosemary. I listened to the birds, I listened to the blackbird, I listened to the trees, I listened to the wind in the branches and the rain on the greenhouse roof. There was tea and biscuit tins, stories and rusty old deckchairs.

*

Stella must have been telling the truth about her back, I did all the bending, the digging and weeding the beds. I dug up the early potatoes and tied in the beans. Every day there was a new surprise. A red flower, a new scent, growth; growth so fast, it was an unstoppable force. Stella stayed mainly in her chair or leaned on the fence. But her spirit didn't fade, she was the sunshine that lighted the day. She loved every flower, every insect, every leaf. She even loved the caterpillars who were eating the cabbages. 'Think of all the butterflies we will have,' she said.

She loved the sun, the clouds and the rain. Even when it rained for twelve days and we couldn't get much done, she told me, 'It's the rain that makes this a green and pleasant land.'

A green and pleasant land. I'd never thought about it that way before. I don't think I ever worried about the rain again. Sitting in the greenhouse, listening to it tap the roof in the afternoon. I never felt happiness till then.

At the end of the summer we collected the seeds into old council envelopes, ready to sow next year.

*

Stella never did get to sow those seeds. It turned out she had been growing a secret of her own. A lump that she wouldn't admit to, that she never complained of. She'd let it take her, like she had let the caterpillars take the cabbages.

Her niece Lucy came down from Scotland to sort out the house and she asked me what I wanted. I took the teapot and the biscuit tin, the spade and the trowel and the packets of seeds. Lucy was a bubble of energy. Wisps of blonde hair fell down a long neck. Blue eyes and a throaty laugh. When I fell in love with her I felt the force of Stella in the place, as if she knew something would grow with Lucy too. Grow after she had gone.

*

Now when I'm in our garden in Scotland with our little boy, I tell him stories. I tell him about carrots and bees. I tell him about rain and villages in Spain. We listen; we listen to the rain; we listen to blackbird and we watch the ants on the apple tree. I watch Lucy as she sits in the old deckchair, growing another baby, growing every day. If it's a girl we will call her Stella.

Angie
by Eric O'Callaghan

Shortlisted, Edinburgh Award for Flash Fiction 2022

Today is the day!
My mind's been racing these past couple of weeks: *Where will we go? What will we do?* Its Angie's last day and I want it to be special. I have a feeling she would love ice cream, but maybe that's just because I love ice cream.

'4 scoops of chocolate please.'

'4 SCOOPS? Be careful little girl, you'll make yourself sick.'

I smile. 'They're not all for me.'

'Do you like ice cream Angie?' Judging by her movements I think she does.

I can't understand why my family don't like her, she's never done anything on them, or anyone.

'She's bad news, cut ties while you can, she'll ruin your life,' they say... but they don't know her.

The ice cream trickles down my fingers as I walk along the pavement. Knowing I've arrived at my destination, I push the door open softly. The debris that blows in from outside creates more of an impression on the room than I do. The women waiting stare at me with sympathy and sorrow melting off their faces, but not the doctor.

'Do you have an appointment?'

'I do sir. Jane Murtagh.'

'Come into my office Jane. How old are you?'

'I'll be fourteen this August sir.'

'Does your family know you're here?'

'They do sir, they're the ones that sent me.'

'Well, okay then. Lay down. This should only take 5 or 10 minutes and it will be gone.'

'She's not an it sir... her name is Angie.'

43 Milliken Lane
by Julie Adams

Longlisted, Scottish Arts Club Short Story Competition 2022

The snow started to settle thickly on the moors just before midday on New Year's Eve. By 2pm, the snowplough driver had called it a day and headed home.

At 4, when Steve Pendergrass drove his van into town, he had to lean so far forward to see through the thick flakes that the seatbelt would be imprinted on his shoulder for days. If he'd known the weather would be like this, he wouldn't have taken the booking. But he'd promised Janet Willoughby a ceilidh band for her 50th birthday, and he wasn't one for letting people down.

In the butcher's, Tommy was preparing to shut up shop. He'd told his boss he'd close at 5.30, but figured nobody in their right mind would be venturing out in this. Unless they were going to the party. But that didn't start till 7.

Further along Main Street, in Betty's Hair Salon, Gemma was sweeping hair off the floor. Careful with that, said Betty, as the broom bashed her Crocs. Gemma muttered an apology, but she wasn't really sorry. Betty didn't pay her enough to deserve a real apology. She couldn't wait to get out of here. Not just the salon; the town. Once she and Tommy had saved enough, they were planning to get the Hell out of Dodge. Six more months. A year at most.

She bent to shovel up the hair and felt a twinge in her stomach. She was starving. She hadn't eaten today because she was saving herself for the buffet at her mum's party. A couple more hours and she could stuff her face with quiche and sausage rolls.

Betty asked her to get Mrs Henderson tea and biscuits. She flicked the switch on the kettle and opened the biscuit barrel. She resisted the urge to fling a few ginger snaps in her mouth, knowing it would ruin her appetite for later. Besides, she'd got into a real bad habit of nibbling biscuits every time she made a cuppa for clients.

No wonder her salon tunic was a lot tighter than when she'd started here.

The Jessop twins ran past the salon. One of them pressed his face against the window and stuck his tongue out. His brother thumped him with a snowball and they ran off laughing.

Outside the community hall, the ceilidh band was unloading their gear from the van. Evan, the caretaker, followed Steve and the other band members into the hall, running through his health and safety checklist. Steve interrupted him to ask where they could get changed. Evan showed him the back room but was annoyed, as he hadn't even pointed out the emergency exits yet.

Across town, near the derelict timber mill, Shauna Burton was holding her phone above her head as though it were an offering to the Gods. After a few moments, she gave up trying to get a signal. Her arm was starting to hurt. She stomped off towards Main Street.

At 14 Laurel Road, Ellen Jones was just arriving home from a 12-hour shift at the hospital. The last thing she needed tonight was to get her glad rags on and go to a ceilidh. But it was her best friend's 50th. So, she couldn't not go. She started running a bath, hoping a long soak, a glass of Malbec and George Michael crooning to her for half an hour would get her in the mood.

Next door, Mrs Wilson, the town's oldest resident was standing in her front porch, looking out at the swirling snow. Lucy, are you out there, she called, her thin, weak voice not carrying more than a foot or two beyond the doorstep. Getting no reply, she tugged her coat on top of her dressing gown and stepped out.

Outside the darkened butcher's shop, Shauna was straining to see in. She rapped hard on the glass, gave it a moment or two, then turned to leave.

Upstairs at 43 Milliken Lane, Janet Willoughby was fixing false eyelashes in front of the bathroom mirror. She took a sip of the espresso martini Dougie had made her and checked her phone to see if anyone else had cancelled. Downstairs, the front door opened and closed. That you, Gemma, she called.

129

Shauna was knocking at Tommy's house. His mum invited her in, but she said she was ok. When he came to the door, she hissed, I've been trying to get hold of you. I think you should tell her tonight. Get it out of the way before the new year. Better if it comes from you. He hesitated, then said, fine, I'll do it before the party.

Back in Milliken Lane, Gemma was barging her way past Janet to get to the toilet. I don't feel well, she said. I need to get to the loo. She slammed the door behind her and Janet called, well don't be long, we're leaving in half an hour.

Ellen was setting her TV to record Jools Holland when she noticed Ellen from next door walking in the middle of the road. She put her glass down and pulled on her boots and jacket.

In the bathroom on Milliken Lane, Gemma was screaming for her mum to come and help her. The door was locked, and it took several attempts before Dougie managed to break it open. When they burst through the doorway Gemma was on all fours, screaming, what's happening to me, over and over.

At the community hall, the caterers were setting up trestle tables for the buffet.

Ellen settled her neighbour in a chair by the fire while she called Mrs Wilson's daughter in Cornwall to let her know she'd found her mum wandering aimlessly in the snow.

Tommy set off towards Milliken Lane, hoping to catch Gemma before she headed out to the party.

And in the distance, blue lights lit up the snow-white moors as an ambulance crawled slowly towards Milliken Lane, where Janet sat in shocked silence, cradling her new-born grandson.

You
by Margaret Callaghan

Shortlisted, Edinburgh Award for Flash Fiction 2022

A face at a conference.
A shared joke.
A lunch turning into evening.
A hand cradling a face.
A kiss under an umbrella.
A body made of silk.
A moving van: two pick-ups, one destination.
A wee house crammed with books.
A shared pair of pyjamas.
A 'defrost the fish' text.
An invite to an engagement party.
A summer of weddings.
A fight about directions (it's never about the directions).
A new baby. Not yours.
A tense family dinner.
An unexpected compliment from a colleague.
A long night where nothing is decided.
A work drink that lasts until the last tube home.
An ultimatum.
A key through a letter box.
A moving van: one pick-up, two destinations.
A warm hand at a muddy graveside.
A late night red wine call.
A short-lived reunion.
A tearful separation and a sudden sense of lightness.
A glimpse on a passing bus.
A box of old postcards.
A like on twitter.
A quick google.

An unexpected obituary in a journal.
A hot knife of grief.

A Shortcut to Nowhere
by Ewan Gault

Longlisted, Scottish Arts Club Short Story Competition 2022

Iona would have cycled past the Jamiesons, but Derrick was in the garden mending a lobster cage.

'Fancy seeing my new place? Got the keys this morning.'

His hands tied and tightened the netting around the trap's entrance, while eyes used to gauging the weight of a catch took in her bare legs and the vintage floral print dress that she hadn't worn since leaving Glasgow.

'Not today.'

His fingers tugged and twisted, fitting the door to the kitchen where the lobsters were lured, twining and tightening the parlour where they'd be caught. The same sullen face, same sunken eyes as his beautiful brother, but hands that were harder, crueller, mindlessly efficient.

'Another time then?'

'Another time.'

She pushed off, knowing he'd be staring at her arse. She'd finished early at the café and cycled along the canal path at a leisurely pace. No point turning up a sweaty mess. It was a sultry still day, the water by her side sheen and sharply reflecting her colourful dress.

Conal Jamieson tilted his trilby and walked to the old winch that had once pulled trawlers onto the beach when the water was wild. The two-hour drive along a road that bucked and bumped like a spooked horse had left him feeling sick, but the salt air seared nostrils, cleared lungs, cleansed head. The squat fisherfolks' houses were hunched and bunched together at the shoreline, as if waiting for their men to come home, their windows staring blindly at the bay.

Is this how he wants her to find him? Slouching next to an old winch, its cogs crusty with rust. Wearing a daft hat and staring off at yachts with their jaunty names and sleek lines, so different from the scabby hulk of his family's lobster boat.

Cycling was good, cycling meant you could approach someone without wondering what to do with your hands. Iona stepped off her bike, head birling as she went for a kiss that smeared his ear. She put his hat on and tussled his hair.

'In disguise?'

'Something like that.'

She remembered a poster of Oscar Wilde's aphorisms on his bedroom wall. *There is only one thing in life worse than being talked about, and that is not being talked about.* And how he'd penned beneath it, *not when you live in the arse end of nowhere.* What he didn't write was that being talked about led to being mocked, spat at, banned from changing rooms, barred from pubs, beaten to a pulp.

She returned the Trilby. 'You didn't stop at your parents?'

*

'I saw your brother on my way over.'

'Fixing lobster traps?'

'Fixing lobster traps.'

Both smiled and without a word stepped over the seaweed slick rocks before clambering up the forest path. They'd done this walk hundreds of times before, but he wasn't wholly hers anymore. A Twitter account with over 4,000 followers, a YouTube channel full of vlogs on exhibitions at London galleries, street fashions, book reviews. Hell, he'd even had articles appear in art quarterlies, and when she'd asked the newsagent if they'd stock them, he'd looked at her as if she was mental.

'Your mum asks after you.'

Conal had held his breath when driving past the cluster of houses by the canal. Eyes fixed on the asphalt, hat pulled low. But even so, his right foot had lifted, his head involuntarily twisted, to see three children playing curbie, the sound of an unfamiliar car that

they knew was never going to turn not interrupting their game.
Conal had travelled down that cul-de-sac plenty of times on Google
street view, swivelled round to stare at the piles of lobster pots in the
garden and the van waiting to take them to the harbour

Castle Dounie was an Iron Age fort from a time when this land
of peninsulas and sea lochs must have seemed worth defending.
Now it was little more than a circular scattering of stones. From up
here ancient people had looked out for unwelcome ships, while
centuries later Conal and Iona had passed endless teenage evenings
drinking, secure in the knowledge that they would see anyone
approaching.

At the top, Conal gulped great draughts of sea breeze, looking
out at Jura, Scarba, a toy sized lobster boat going to sea.

'I miss big horizons.'

'You get used to them.'

Amongst the kelp-coloured collage of sea and islands, beneath
a mottled and spotted seal grey sky, the only house was the tiny
sugar cube cottage on the Northern tip of Jura where Orwell wrote
1984. This was the original reason they came here. Not for its
splendid isolation — there was no shortage of places with that — but
to feel a connection with this bit of literature that came out of their
deserted land.

'Madness. Coming all this way to write a book.'

'Was he not paranoid about being spied on in London?'

'Nah, he was scared there'd be a nuclear war.'

'And he thought Jura would be safe?'

'What's there to bomb on Jura? It'd be a waste of a nuke.'

Iona unpacked the picnic, amused by his bitterness. This had
held them together. Sitting up places with a view and scathingly
scouring the scenery.

She produced sandwiches and a Tupperware box filled with
flapjacks, fairycakes and millionaire's shortbread, the recipe for each
never having changed since her mother's time. How did it feel,
morning after morning following the fading ink of your mother's

handwritten instructions, measuring out the same quantity of flour, the same number of eggs, as she had for decades of her life? It was two years since the funeral. Asked at the last minute to be a pall bearer — she'd always had a soft spot for him — the eyes of the congregation on the electric blue nail polish he hadn't the time to clean off. 'A bloody disgrace,' his father had called him. 'Making a spectacle of yourself at that good woman's burial.'

'How are things at the café?'

'Do you know what *1984*'s working title was? The last man in Europe. Most days I can relate to that. The apocalypse could've happened and we wouldn't notice.'

Some days she'd drop a cup just to hear it smash. And then feel bad, because every piece of crockery had been washed and dried by her mother's hands. The endless hours looking out at the canal — 'Scotland's most beautiful shortcut' — constructed by men driven off their land, who needed to be put to work, as there was nothing more dangerous than a person with time on their hands. They had no photos of these men on the café's wall, but the rest of the canal's history was there: a steamer carrying Queen Victoria, puffer boats bringing goods from industrial Scotland to the islands, tourists going from Glasgow on their holidays for the dancing when this was more likely to be done on Islay than Ibiza, Mull than Majorca.

'I thought some millionaire passing by on his yacht would have whisked you off by now.'

She scowled. There were plenty of that sort. Men with straight teeth and floppy hair, gilets and red trousers. Loud and excitable men, who fell silent when she approached with their coffee and cakes. Her father loved taking them over the shipping maps. That had always been his forte. Front of house, endlessly affable, a great memory for names, even though he would sometimes stare at her as if he'd seen a ghost.

'You know, there's a couch at mine with your name on it.'

And that had always been their plan, but six months working in her parents' café after graduating became twelve and even the tips she hoarded from serving snacks and snippets of information about the local area had never been enough. And now it was too late.

'You don't need to keep on for your dad's sake. There are others who could do your job.'

But that was only part of the problem. How disappointed he'd be if he knew. The sort of stupid situation daft girls at school with no ambition got trapped in. And with his brother too. His dull-as-fuck stay at home big brother, who believed that any man who didn't do a manual job, who actively sought out music that wasn't on the radio, who read anything that wasn't to do with mechanics was *suspect* and very possibly a homosexual. At one time she'd thought Conal's entire personality had been created just to piss off his brother.

He'd done well to get away. She followed his life on Instagram. A world in which everyone was under 30, artfully dishevelled and always drinking while never looking drunk. Broadband hadn't reached their hamlet and she'd wander down the towpath to a wall by the harbour hotel to use their Wi-Fi. With fingers numbed by winds that had howled across the North Atlantic, she'd scroll through his photos, count his likes.

She watched Conal's hands as he talked about some art installation in a skyscraper and thought of his brother. That night at the start of summer. The May Day Bank Holiday — the first evening it'd been warm enough to have a barbecue — and in the gloaming and glow from the charcoal, he'd looked so much like Conal. She'd worked a 12-hour shift and glugged gladly at whatever was put in her hand. Derrick stirred the charcoal, put more lobster on the grill. His hands at work, well-shaped like his brothers. He told her stories from the sea: a naked man spotted meditating amongst the midges on a deserted island; peering in the windows of the abandoned mansion at Inch Kenneth where Unity Mitford hid out during the war; being paid two hundred pounds to sail a priest to a wedding on Scarba because the other skippers were too superstitious to let a clergyman on their boats. Mr Jamieson was letting him take over the business side of things and he had plans.

'You'll be looking for a wife soon,' she'd smirked and he'd looked at her, the way Conal used to when she'd said something that unsettled the equilibrium of their friendship. It was then he'd picked up a lobster pot that needed mending, had explained to her how the creatures thought they were crawling into a comfy wee house. He'd thrust his hand through the funnel into a part of the trap called the kitchen. Told her about the best bait to use and how, once they'd had their fill, the lobsters would try to leave, but would find themselves trapped in an inner chamber called the parlour.

*

At his hire car they hugged goodbyes. Could he feel the curve of her belly as she promised to visit?

'Don't just visit. This,' he gestured at the coastline, 'Is beautiful, but it's not really a life.'

As he turned the key in the ignition, she remembered Sunday nights getting the train from their Pollokshields flat they'd shared through university. Dressed up for a night at the Sub Club, rolling onto the platform at Glasgow Central, past the couples saying goodbye to another weekend before one of them climbed onto the last train for London. Back then she'd been so sure they would never let life separate them like that. Back then she'd do his eyeliner, sure he loved her too, and that all this camping about was just a rebellious joke.

She cycled along the canal in a daze. At the Jamiesons, the lobster traps were mended and stacked, ready to be dropped into the ocean. From behind a steamed window, the blurry outline of Mrs Jamieson preparing dinner amidst the dull percussion of pot lids and pans. Tomorrow, she would get the bus to Glasgow, go with Conal down to London and escape all this. Surely, she could do that?

Reaching out to touch the knots and netting of the trap she felt life quicken inside her.

Just a walk in the Park
by Macleay Lindsay

Shortlisted, Edinburgh Award for Flash Fiction 2022

Sunday 16th

Dear Peter, thank you for bringing Clare home after the fall, it was kind and generous of you and much appreciated by Clare, as she was really shaken up by the incident.

I do not think that your dog Wally is really to blame, as dogs will be dogs. He was only chasing the ball you had thrown in an entirely different direction.

It was more, I think, the race between Wally and Coco, and I am sure you'll agree that Coco is a very big and very clumsy boisterous dog. Both dogs racing for the ball is a dangerous combination, which has plainly eventuated.

Clare is sleeping now, and I trust things will be OK in the morning.

Warm regards, John.

Monday 17th

Dear Peter, I have taken Clare to the hospital as the Doctor felt that it's better to be sure than sorry. A couple of X-rays and tests. He was a little concerned about the fall.

Although you said she didn't lose consciousness, such falls are always potentially dangerous and the collision of the dogs was pretty forceful, and unexpected, coming from behind.

Anyway, I will keep you informed.

Regards, John.

Wednesday 19th

Dear Peter, I have been advised that it is appropriate to seek formal advice on this matter. I understand that you will be covered by the public liability clause in your insurance.

My Lawyer is Andrew Alberts of Alberts and Alberts.
John.

Friday 21st
Dear Peter Brown,
Send flowers.
John Smith

The Last Tram
by Frank Carter

Longlisted, Scottish Arts Club Short Story Competition 2022

The boy and his mother sit by the fire in the kitchen. She knits and talks to herself, her face telling him something of what she feels about what she's thinking. He thinks: she is content and she is occupied and not about to pack him off to bed. So he sits quiet, quiet with his two National Geographic magazines, the ones he's found in the attic box that he was allowed to open, the box which belonged to his father, where he kept things from the War. The boy might not be allowed to stay up with his Wizard or Hotspur, but with National Geographics, he can. His mother has said he can look at the magazines, look at the maps, charts and the awesome photographs; and she'll read out what he cannot manage. So long as he's very careful with the magazines; they are older than he is and must be taken special care of. Like this: the pair of them sitting by the fire; both busy with what they like doing. The boy feels his mother is not exasperated with him, just now. Exasperated. The boy has learned the word but does not really know what it is about himself that she finds exasperating. Maybe it's because there's only him and her nowadays. 'You can be so exasperating,' she often says.

The front-door bell rings.

'Who can that be?' His mother looks up, startled. 'And at this time o' night. You'd better go see who it is and bring them in out of the cold. Don't let the cold in, mind.'

The boy has been staring fascinated at the Murchison Falls, crocodiles taking wildebeests, the aurora borealis, a solitary bear cub ploughing after its mother over snow-clad Rocky Mountains, another world. His reverie is interrupted. But he likes there being someone at the door.

He needs no second bidding; off he goes, closing the kitchen door behind him to keep the warm in, he skips down the hallway to the front door. The light from the hall shines through the window pane in the door on to the door step, where stands a familiar figure.

'Uncle Billy!'

'Aye, lad, 's me right enough.'

Uncle Billy is Mr Rae from the terrace next door. 'A wiz jist wantin' tae use yer mither's phone. An' maybe you are just the very lad to use the phone for me.'

'Yes, yes. Come in out of the cold.' Uncle Billy is wearing what he calls his 'auld woolie' and flat cap, both showing signs of snow.

'Naw, lad, I'll bide here an' see the trams pass along. There's the 18 and the 26 keep comin' but she's no back yet. No hame after a' this time. It's snowin' heavy now, gettin' late and she's no hame. No hame yet.'

The boy listens. He feels the cold, the concern, something's wrong. Gone wrong. Going wrong. 'Here's another tram,' he says. Mr Rae steps out of the shelter of the front porch on to the gravel path, the better to see down the drive, down to the High Street where the tram cars pass. This tram stops at the foot of the drive.

But if anyone does get on or get off, the snow keeps that to itself. No-one appears to walk round the corner onto their street... and up to the doorstep where Mr Rae and the boy are standing. Uncle Billy watches the tram, the boy watches Uncle Billy. No-one.

Only the snow and the trams and the waiting.

'You want the phone, Uncle Billy?'

'Aye, A do that. She's been a' day wi' thon auld crone, Maisie Colquoun. Here's her number; A've written it doon.' He hands a slip of paper to the boy. 'Want you to phone the auld besom and check oot if Mrs Rae has left Largs yet.' He hands the boy a sixpence.

The boy is pleased to help, knowing what Uncle Billy thinks of the telephone. He returns to the hall, closing the front door behind him. Keeps the cold out. The telephone is on the table by the hallstand. He drops Uncle Billy's sixpence into the glass jar by the phone; that's too much, he thinks. But Uncle Billy must be worried.

142

The boy lifts the big, shiny receiver, as he has been taught, and waits.

'Number please?'

The boy checks the slip of paper. 'Largs four-nine-five-o,' he intones. 'Nasty, winter's night,' says the operator. And the boy agrees, feeling very grown up. There's a moment's silence followed by 'brrrr... brrrr...' and again.

Then... 'Hello, who's this? What do you want?'

'It's me, Mrs Colquoun. Uncle Billy wants to know if Mrs Rae has left you yet.'

'Och, it's just you, is it. You should be in yer bed. Tell that old fool the phone'll no bite. Gettin' a boy to use the phone when... Aye, she's left a while since; I saw her on to the Glasgow train, the six-minutes-past-seven, like always. She should be home by this time.'

'Thank you. I'll go tell him.'

'Aye and tell him the phone will no bite.'

The line goes dead. He replaces the receiver on its cradle. Babies have cradles. But phones? He is quick to rejoin Uncle Billy, closing the door behind him. He imparts Mrs Colquoun's message — only the train bit.

'Here comes another,' says Uncle Billy. But the tram doesn't stop.

The boy feels Uncle Billy's disappointment; he stands close beside him. Like he does at the rugby, when Mr Rae takes the boy by train to Murrayfield to watch Scotland. Where Uncle Billy joins forces with his old pals from the Borders where he was brought up. Where he and the boy meet Sandy and Jock, farmers from Selkirk, and the Hawick butcher. 'Mind, there'll be no bad language,' Uncle Billy reminds his friends. 'No in front of the boy.' The men nod earnestly.

The Hawick butcher looks at the boy, sheepish-like, the boy thinks, and wonders: what language is bad language? French maybe, or Italian?

143

When yet another tram comes and goes — they hear it before they see it — the boy asks Uncle Billy: has he any tomatoes left? He always helps Uncle Billy plant out his tomatoes from the greenhouse; he'll taste a few, the wee ones; pick out the unwanted shoots and gather the crop, even late into the year.

'Naw, lad, they's a' gone. Mrs Rae pickled the last o' them. Must gie you an' yer mither a jar o' her green tomato chutney. It's real champion.'

'It'll be real champion, right enough,' says the boy, echoing Uncle Billy.

They see the lights of the next tram car though the bare branches of the wood across the street, hear it jolting and juddering up the High Street. Doesn't stop. The boy wants something else to say.

Snow rests on Uncle Billy's garden fence. 'Your fence looks great. You did a grand job there.'

'Aye. We done a grand job, right enough, you and me.'

The boy remembers. He helped when Uncle Billy was painting his garden fence two Sundays ago. He holds the brushes; when Uncle Billy finishes with the big brush he hands it to the boy who swaps it for the wee brush. Pastor McSween appears. He lives two doors up and is on his way to the Kirk, bible tucked under one arm, sermon smouldering under his collar. He crosses the drive but pauses midway, 'I was just minded to think, Mr Rae, the world would be a far, far better place if some of us would spend as much time worshipping the Lord on the Sabbath, as we do painting our fences.'

Uncle Billy takes the wee brush from the boy, half turns towards Pastor McSween, 'Aye, an' I was jist minded to think, Mr McSween, the world would be a far, far better place if some of us would just mind oor own business.'

It's getting late. The snow thicker, the night colder. The boy has counted three more empty trams. He has an idea, 'Uncle Billy,

144

would you be wantin' a mug of tea?' He feels the man's hand on his head, ruffling his hair, 'Aye, lad, A would that. That'd be just...'

'Champion,' boy and man say together.

The boy hurries through to the kitchen and into the scullery, closing doors behind him. His mother is counting her stitches. 'Och, you,' she says, 'look what you've made me do.' She restarts: one, two... five, six... He notices the time on the mantelpiece: ten-past-ten.

'I'm putting the kettle on,' says the boy, not wanting to exasperate her — again — and tea, he knows, always works.

Uncle Billy has given the boy a mug with his initials on it 'BR'. Which, he has explained, stands for Billy Rae and not necessarily for British Rail, where he has worked all his life. The boy understands.

He boils the kettle on the gas, four rounded teaspoons of tea in the pot, two heaped teaspoons of sugar in the mug marked BR. He doesn't forget his mother, who is pleased to receive a cuppa when her knitting is causing her issues; she smiles at the boy. Then has to start counting again.

He leaves her quickly, quietly and takes careful steps with his full mug of steaming tea through to Uncle Billy. He holds the mug by the handle and reaches out to Uncle Billy, who is squinting through the falling snow. The boy opens his eyes as wide as he can when he is watching, not like Uncle Billy. He tries squinting too. They peer together, eyes straining, wanting and waiting. Mr Rae takes the mug in a large paw and sips his tea. He appears not bothered by the hot or the cold, the boy can tell.

The tea makes its mark.

Uncle Billy sips and sighs, and he looks at the boy, who is watching him, who is with him. 'There'll be no many more trams now. An' see, there's no buses the night, no traffic at a', only the trams.' The boy sees. There is another tram coming though. They see it before they hear anything, all sounds being muffled in the snow. The tram's lights flicker and stutter up the High Street. It ghosts to a stop.

145

The boy feels something being draped around his shoulders. His mother has left her knitting and her tea and come to the front step. His father's tweed jacket, which has always hung on the hallstand, is wrapped around the boy.

At the bottom of the street something moves.

The curtain of snow parts just enough to reveal a shape. A small figure, slow and deliberate, plods heavily up the pavement, footprints black in the snow, like the tracks of the bear cub, the boy thinks. He feels his heart pump, deep under his father's jacket. Uncle Billy has stepped over into his own garden, 'Aye, well,' he says. The figure has made it to their gate and can be heard chuntering to itself. Uncle Billy has always said: she aye likes to talk.

'A've never been sae fed up in a' ma life.' She rambles on about trains being held up on Fenwick Moor and the freezin' cold and the guard and the night. Uncle Billy intervenes, 'Well, A telt ye.'

He turns towards the boy and his mother, hands over the tea mug, 'Thankee kindly,' he says. 'You have a grand lad there, Missus.' The boy's feet are cold, his hands are cold, his face is cold; inside, he is warm.

Uncle Billy wraps his arm about Mrs Rae, who disappears into his auld woolie. He pushes his own front-door open. 'Come away in,' he says.

Seas the Day
by Ann Seed

Shortlisted, Edinburgh Award for Flash Fiction 2022

'Perfect,' my younger son, Gordie, said.

And so it was. Bow waves dancing to the engine's throaty hum... a balming breeze bouncing diamonds on the sea... and there... the isle of Mull... shining like a slice of Heaven in the gossamer light…

The ferry docked at Craignure and we drove off. I nearly choked with anticipation, with the idyll that the day might bring.

'Where do you think?' Gordie asked, deferring to Rob's status as the older brother.

Perhaps Calgary Bay, I thought. Wild... open... Coll beckoning to the west... to the south, the puffin haven of the Treshnish Isles. I longed for Iona too... and Staffa to its north where basalt columns march into giant sea caves. Please not Tobermory though... the harbour is too busy...

But it was the boys' decision, their day. I would go wherever they wished. Mull had been my idea but otherwise they had free reign. I noticed they'd put a picnic basket in the car boot. And a hip flask. Full of malt whisky no doubt. For later, I hoped, when the driving... the day... was done.

It turned out to be the small isle of Ulva. A brief foot-ferry ride off the west coast. I had been there once, had raved about the peace, its other-worldliness.

My sons found a good spot, unscrewed the lid, tipped up the urn...

I glittered with the diamonds on the waves... breathed in the joy... the endless possibilities of the oceans beyond...

Perfect.

Crescendo
by Ken Cohen

Longlisted, Scottish Arts Club Short Story Competition 2022

Ben sits alone on the edge of the table in the brightly lit room, his feet not quite touching the ground. Unable to sit still, fizzing with nervous energy, he swings his legs back and forth. He knows there's nothing left but to wait. He also knows waiting is his nemesis.

He tries composing himself by focusing on his breathing. Deep breath in; count slowly to five; deep breath out. It should calm him, but it doesn't. No matter how much he attempts to concentrate, he only becomes more conscious of what lies ahead.

Ben looks at the clock on the wall.

Ten minutes.

His life will change. One way or another — in ten minutes, the door will open, and he'll be summoned. He'll follow the usher down a long, narrow, dimly lit corridor. He'll tremble as each step takes him closer — closer to the moment for which he's been preparing his whole life. Ben hopes, when the time comes, he'll be able to stand; that his legs will be strong enough to support him; that he'll be able to plant his feet firmly on the ground and walk assuredly down the corridor; that he won't add embarrassment to anxiety by tripping and falling over his own feet.

Nine minutes.

Ben thinks of the path that brought him here. Of the long hours of disciplined practice shut away from the sunshine when his friends played football or cricket or idled away their time during the long summer holidays.

'Coming to the park today, Ben?' Josh would ask as he stood on the doorstep, his bike propped against the front hedge.

'Not today, Josh!'

'You still practicing, then?'

'Yeah! Still practicing!'

'OK then! Maybe tomorrow?'

'Maybe tomorrow!'

Ben remembers how Josh would turn, mount his bike and cycle off down the road to meet up with the rest of the gang. How he longed to escape his confinement and join them.

He closes his eyes and swings his legs more vigorously. Not sure why, he finds himself thinking of the photos that adorn the living room walls. Just to the left of the clock, there's one of the shy, earnest looking boy he once was; a seven year old, deep in concentration, violin tucked firmly under his chin, fingers riding deftly up and down the neck of the instrument playing the *Prelude in D* by Shostakovich. In the background, his mother accompanies him on the piano at his first public performance. To the right of the clock he recalls another larger photo; now he's aged ten and still just as earnest. Here, for the first time, at last, he's standing in front of an orchestra. He remembers the moment with great pride and satisfaction. He thinks of how the Bruch *Violin Concerto in G Minor* opens, with that gentle timpani roll followed by the short woodwind phrase. He thinks of how he counted the bars until the time came to draw his bow across the strings, to make his slow, rich, confident entry. And he thinks of the other photo. There! On the other side of the room. A recent shot of him brimming with joy, his mother and father grinning on either side bursting with pride. He pictures how he tightly clutched his Young Violinist of the Year award as if any relaxation of his grip would send it falling to the ground, shattering into a thousand tiny splinters.

Seven minutes.

Ben stands, tugs at his tuxedo, adjusts his bow tie and bends to polish his shoes for perhaps the hundredth time. He hates wearing a tuxedo.

'It looks so professional. It conveys just the right impression,' his mother keeps telling him. The impresario concurs.

But really! A fifteen-year-old in a tuxedo? Besides, it's physically restrictive. The top button of his crisp white shirt is done up and the bow tie feels tight around his neck. Once he places the violin under his chin, the collar will cut into his skin and the sleeves of his jacket will ride high and tug tight around his upper arms and under his armpits making it awkward to draw the bow easily across the strings. If only he could wear jeans and a tee-shirt! Then he'd have a chance of playing his best!

Six minutes.

Ben hates being last. Not just because of the long wait, but because as each contestant plays with technical brilliance and an emotional maturity that belies their years, audience expectations will be heightened; they always expect the best to be last and this time, Ben is not so sure he is the best. And much as he tries, he cannot banish the nagging doubts that keep surfacing; how can he ever match his performance at the competition he won just weeks before; when he'd closed his eyes, trusted his instincts, lost himself in the music and played flawlessly with all the passion his fifteen years could muster?

There was always something to practice.

There was always something he could improve.

There was always some small thing that had to be corrected.

There was always something about his play that wasn't quite ready for public performance.

Five minutes.

Ben turns his attention to the music, Tchaikovsky. He's practiced it so many times with his teacher he now knows every note well enough. Every bar, every crotchet, every quaver committed to memory. In just a few short moments, he'll be standing in front of a full orchestra, facing the conductor and the audience, conscious the television cameras under the glaring lights will catch not just his performance but his every gesture, every action, every flicker of the eyelid, every nervous reflex, every tiny bead of sweat.

Everything. As if under a microscope. To be studied. Judged.

150

All instantly beamed to millions of viewers.

And if his mask slips, how will they not see it; the terror behind his eyes; the trepidation that has lain concealed all these years in the pit of his stomach?

Four minutes.

Ben is alone. It isn't as if it's the first time. He should be used to it, but he isn't. These moments are moments of intensity; it's an ordeal he bears less well as each performance comes and goes.

He thinks again of the music. It's all that can lift his spirits. He considers the opening bars. A short 30 second introduction by the strings joined by the woodwind, all reaching a frenzied crescendo even before the first minute is out; the two sections in competition with each other for attention before a diminuendo and a brief moment of silence. A moment in time when all eyes will be on him. A moment of intense anticipation.

Ben thinks of the first violins who will be seated so close to where he'll be standing in just a few moments. How could he think his performance will be comparable to these experienced professionals, whose technique, maturity and emotional interpretation so surely outweigh his own?

What if he misses his cue?

What if he makes a mistake in the very first bar?

What if he can't recover?

What if his performance has already peaked?

What if...?

One minute.

Ben adjusts his tie once more. He slicks back his hair and closes his eyes, thinking of the music he must conjure; of the emotions he must stir. He feels caged and suddenly wants to run. Maybe he'll climb through the window, out into the cold winter air and run into the night. He could run from the concert hall to the street. He could somehow seek refuge in the crowds, even dressed as he is in his black tuxedo. He even goes to the window and tries it. But it's almost as if someone has predicted his flight. The window is locked. He's trapped.

The door opens. Ben takes a deep breath. It's time. It's time for him to plant his feet firmly on the ground, to walk assuredly down the long, narrow, dimly lit corridor, each step taking him closer to the moment for which he has so long been working. Now, he can hear the chatter from the audience. It grows louder as he approaches. Standing in the wings, he can see each instrumentalist waiting, seated behind music stands. Some tune their instruments. Others turn the pages of their sheet music. They all look calm, even cheerful, as if this is just a matter of routine. Which Ben supposes it is. For them. None of them can surely feel the rising tide of nausea he feels as he realises there is now no turning back.

Ben walks onto the stage and is instantly blinded by the stage lighting which mercifully blocks his view of all but the first two rows of the audience. He is deafened by the applause and daunted by the thought it is all for him. Summoning all his courage, he bows uncomfortably, his tuxedo tightening around his chest and shoulders. He stands upright, then takes his position. He shifts his gaze back and forth between the conductor and the orchestra leader watching for the cues, shutting out anything that might distract him.

The conductor raises his baton and silently cuts it through the air. As if by magic, the strings respond with the first strains of Tchaikovsky's *Violin Concerto in D*. As the baton traces giant pictures before him, the bows rise and fall in unison with exquisite grace and beauty. Thirty seconds in and perfectly on time, the woodwind follow, at once competing with the violins for attention. Here is the crescendo; there is the diminuendo. Now, a minute in, he is deeply immersed in the music.

Ben tucks his violin under his chin. He holds his bow ready. There is everything to play for; everything to lose. Yet there's still a nagging doubt lingering in his mind; what if he's not good enough? What if his last win was his last ever win? Of one thing he's certain; his life will never be the same again.

The conductor nods at Ben, raises his beckoning hand and points his baton. It's time.

The Sound of Music
by Andy Raffan

Shortlisted, Edinburgh Award for Flash Fiction 2022

See Dad said it was lending not forever cos the man didnae have anything to play his music wi'. Ah said could ah wear ma blue dress an' Dad laughed but no' with his eyes an' said aye if ye're quick. So ah put it on even though it's tight now, and ma good shoes too even though they nip ma toes. Then ah carried the bit you put the seedees in, an' Ryan carried the speakers cos they're light an' he's only six, but we had to tape the wires to the back so he didnae trip. Ah felt all proud that everyone could see us walkin' to the shop with the big yellow sign to do such a good deed. Me an' Ryan waited outside for Dad, an' when he came out he said he was goin' to see a man about a dug. Ah really, really hope that means we're gonnae get a puppy even though Mum always says stop askin' we cannae afford one.

She came home when we were in bed an' there was shouting for a while then the front door went bang. Ah came through an' Mum was putting all her seedees in a bin bag an' cryin'. So ah started to sing a bit from one of her favourites about shining bright like a diamond an' she grabbed me an' squeezed so tight ah had to stop so maybe it isnae one of her favourites after all.

The Two Gems
by Kate Blackadder

Shortlisted, Edinburgh Award for Flash Fiction 2022

We moved house five times last year. A new name, a new history to remember.

Move number four. October. At school I was put beside a girl called Gemma. I was being Gemma then and this other one gave me the smiliest smile ever.

She shared her bag of crisps every breaktime and we called ourselves 'the two Gems'.

I wasn't supposed to make friends. I wasn't supposed to go to other girls' houses. But when Gemma asked me I went to hers.

Her dad had made her a tree house. I wished I could stay up there forever.

Her mum gave us hot chocolate and her house had shelves of books like at Granny's.

I used to sit behind the sofa and read, trying not to hear Mum crying and Granny saying, leave him, and Mum saying, you don't understand.

'How nice for Gemma to have a friend called Gemma!' her mum said.

'I'm not really Gemma,' I told her. Then I told her everything because she was so nice and because it's so muddling always being someone else.

I hoped she might ask me to come and live with them, like happened to orphans in books. But of course I wasn't an orphan so instead she walked me home and came inside to speak to Mum.

When she'd gone Mum packed our bags.

That's when I was ten. I know better than to make friends, now that I'm eleven.

My name is Alice now.

The Disappearing
by Hilary Plews

Longlisted, Scottish Arts Club Short Story Competition 2022

Last night you dream of Archie. You feel as though he's right beside you, but in some other place. You wake up, distressed, after a crow urges you to remember where you have been and what passed between you with an eerie combination of sympathetic hostility. The dream's within grasping distance, and then it evaporates, like mist.

You don't tell your twin sister that the loss of a beloved lessens with time (even though you know from experience that it does), and you'd feel stupid telling her anything even slightly comforting when her husband maybe isn't dead, but is definitely vanished. You come to stay every Christmas, the anniversary. The story's always the same: early morning Boxing Day beach stroll and never returns. You are unsure whether, or if, such memorialising makes sense. Seven years pass. Cassie's coping, but only so-so. The kids, now sixteen and nineteen do better, although you notice that the younger, Sam, confuses his tenses when speaking of Archie. And why not? No-one, not even the police, know if Sam's dad is or was. There may be one person, you think, who might know, but the police eventually rule out murder because there's no body. There's no obvious motive either; everyone agrees Archie was thoroughly decent, and even his international business colleagues and competitors have nothing bad to say.

Not that the tabloids care about any of the facts. Cassie wears all the headlines, like so many hand-me-downs. They range from *Grieving Widow* to *Archie the Amnesiac* sighted in various unlikely places via *McRae the Russian spy* and *Missing Husband in Love Triangle Mystery* with yet more foreign 'sightings'. It's gruelling. They come to live with you in Brighton for a while, as far as possible from their home in North Berwick. But Cassie's beautiful, her children equally photogenic, the press are omnipresent and the apparent hunger for tragedy so immense that the family can't slip out of the juggernaut's intrusive, steamrollering attention. With the help of your networks, some hair dye, and hippy clothes, you finally magic them away with you to the Isle of Wight and a remote cottage, presided over by a large bull of a farmer.

You're needed at the North Berwick anniversaries to field the press who *still* occasionally pop up, sprouting crocodile tears and offers of cash to unravel the comfort that any of them may have acquired since the disappearing. That's what they call it. Present continuous. What is disappearing may reappear, like the setting sun. Disappearance sounds too final, too dead. His friends say, he would never have knowingly disappeared without a word, and that he was as likely to have been a foreign spy as Baroness Hale. As for an illicit affair, which the police favour as the key to the tragedy, Archie and secrets go together like marmite and jelly. Isn't that so? Cassie demands. Don't you remember I had to give up telling him what we'd bought the boys for Christmas, because he always spilled the beans. You do not share Cassie's belief in Archie's inability to keep secrets, but as to what really happened, you are as mystified as anyone else, although you favour the random killer theory. Favour is not the right word, but there is no right word for what you have done. This anniversary's different, because being the seventh year, Cassie files and gets a Declarator of Death from the sheriff's court. She is now officially a widow. She has looked into the never-ending chasm of the present continuous and decides to side with death. To end it, she says, so that we can be reborn.

Cassie worries about Stuart, the eldest. He's doing OK at uni, or so he says, but he rarely utters at home. You are her ambassador so you knock on his door. He's strewn across his bed with various bits of electronic equipment sprouting out of him. He looks up and nods. He removes his gigantic headphones. You attempt small talk. You give up on small talk. You look out of the window and admire, yet again, the stunning sea view. You practise silence, not your

157

strong point, but Stuart can do silence better than a Trappist monk, so you take a deep breath,

'How are you doing, this anniversary?'

'Aye, fine.'

'Meaning?'

'Fine. You know.'

'A-ha.' You have to think past Stuart's block. He used to be such a chatterbox. 'What would have to change for things to be good?'

He looks at you with a mixture of contempt and pity.

You shrivel. 'Sorry, stupid question... so... what are your plans?'

He shrugs.

'I mean, are you still wanting a career in engineering?'

'Mebbe.'

You give up and retreat, shaking your head when Cassie looks at you expectantly. Her eyes fill with tears. She is holding the delicate whale tooth scrimshaw she thinks Archie found for her in an Edinburgh antique shop.

You make yourself useful by taking Sam to see his mate. You persuade Cassie to come for a walk. She doesn't want to leave Stuart on his own in case the press come, but you point out that he'll not hear a thing wearing those headphones. The tide is out and it takes ages before you can both paddle. Crows crowd the hard, dark sand, like so many bad-ass lawyers. You walk for an age in one direction, then the other. The sea hisses and whispers and freezes your bare feet until they get used to the chill and you talk.

'Do you ever dream of him?' she asks.

'No,' you reply, a little too quickly. 'Do you?'

'All the time,' she says. 'I quite like it.'

'What happens?' You feel you have to ask.

'Nothing much. We hang out. Visit places we went to when we were young. It's comforting. Sometimes we have sex. Great sex.'

Oh God, you think, but don't say.

'I thought they would stop after the 'Presumption of Death' thing, but they haven't. He's aged — just like he would have if he'd still been with us. And he's wearing glasses. Little round things, like John Lennon.' Cassie laughs. She's brightened up.

You force a smile, unsure whether what she's telling you is normal. You wend your way back through the sand dunes, dislodging the odd twitcher as you go. They look as shifty as the crows. You stop in your tracks, suddenly struck by something Cassie has said. Shiiit, you think, but don't say, when Cassie asks if anything's the matter. You sit side by side on a rock to put on your socks and boots and stamp some life back into your frozen feet. You both stare at the waves, now on the turn and beginning the long haul back to their debris-spangled high tide mark.

'Nothing's the matter,' you lie.

She slips her arm through yours. 'It really helps that you come up every anniversary. Christmas would be hell without you, you know.'

You do know, but you don't want to. You're a fraud.

You can't sleep that night because the little round specs have wedged themselves in your mind. Archie was wearing a pair in your dream. You are not superstitious; there is no meaning in this. Archie was just the kind of man who would buy a pair of John Lennon specs as age diminished his 20:20 vision. A shadowy crow hops around the edge of your consciousness, ensuring that sleep is banished. You haul yourself downstairs to make a cup of tea. Stuart sits at the kitchen table, eating his way through a mountain of toast. It smells delicious, but he doesn't offer you any. There surely can't be anything left of the loaf.

'He fancied you, didn't he?'

'Come again?' you say, feigning sleepiness, but instantly alert.

'Dad.'

'Ye-es, I-I think he did.' Your aim is to convey embarrassment.

159

'Wanker. He knew you were gay.'

'Well,' you say, 'I think that can be an attraction. Ridiculous, but there you are.'

'I suppose that can work both ways?' Stuart mutters, eyes turned hard as pebbles.

You deem it best to pretend you have not heard. Your nephew returns to gnawing his last piece of toast. You sit down opposite him with your tea, and keep your shaking hands under the table. He isn't finished.

'That must have made visiting us a wee bit... ehm... tricky.'

'Nooo. I made my position very clear.' You watch Stuart minutely, behind the hand covering a fake yawn.

'Mum doesn't know,' he says.

'No,' you agree.

There is a silence. You know you must not be the first to break it.

'So you and he...?'

'Stuart — *no!* Nothing happened.'

He looks relieved. Probably not as relieved as you feel. He gets up, crumbs scatter. 'Wanker,' he repeats, before heading for the stairs.

Your tea has become cold. You sip it anyway to calm your pounding chest. You should have been an actress. Archie wasn't the only wanker, you think.

*

Courtesy of your job, you cannot attend the eighth anniversary, for which you are heartily grateful. You have often wondered how Stuart found out as much as he did, because you never thought of him as being particularly observant. And you were so careful. Perhaps the disappearing was a God-send after all? You shake your head to rid yourself of such a selfish thought and find yourself being stared at by a crow who has perched on the railing of your hotel balcony. You find it hard to tear your two eyes away from his merciless glare. A single black eye glints in the afternoon sun and

160

peers deep into the putrid mess of what passes for your soul. When you finally tear yourself away from the balcony door, the crow caws, a jarring, scornful sound.

The National Geographic has sent you to El Caño in Coclé province, Panama to photo the bodies being excavated from a pre-Columbian cemetery. The Chief, as he emerges from layers of exposed earth, and the unfortunate table of human remains supporting him beneath, drips gold. From his carved breastplate to his belt, armbands and necklace, gold festoons his body like a second skin. Exquisite brooches are also unearthed carved with fantastical creatures – half human and half entirely other. The gold is extraordinary, but the find that moves you, is the belt made from a whale's teeth. You hope Cassie will be distracted by your photos of this and those in which the tropical sun transforms the gold-adorned chief to fire.

As you are paying off your fare outside Panama City's Departures Terminal, your attention is caught by the family hurrying to catch the taxi up front. The woman carries a toddler and her hair is piled up on her beautiful head, somewhat obscuring the following husband who pushes a reluctant luggage trolley. All three are laughing as the driver stows their bags, and the man opens the rear door for his wife and child. Whilst they pile in, he removes a handkerchief from his jeans pocket and vigorously polishes his glasses. They aren't John Lennon specs, but the body owning them is, you are quite certain, that of Archie McRae. As if to confirm it, the man side steps into the taxi with the graceful slide you remember so well, bangs the door shut and they are driven away.

Cassie will hear no word of this from you, but it turns out that she already knows. She collects you from North Berwick station and bursts into tears in the car.

'We needed you, this last anniversary, we so did. The press came. After all this time. They said sources thought Archie was living in — oh, somewhere in Latin America, Stuart will remember,

161

under an assumed name. That he has another family. This can't be true. Tell me it can't be. Cannot, CANNOT be.'

You hold Cassie in your arms. 'Archie is dead,' you say.

Double Espresso
by Sally Arkinstall

Shortlisted, Edinburgh Award for Flash Fiction 2022

I was halfway down my second cappuccino before he arrived. The bag containing his toothbrush and spare clothes was on the seat beside me. I would return his things after I'd explained that it was over.

'I'm so sorry I'm late.' Familiar words oozed from him. 'It took longer than I expected to get here.'

I said nothing, I didn't want a fight. It always took longer than he expected.

He looked at his watch. 'I haven't got long. I'm meeting Martin at half past; I don't want to keep him waiting.'

'I need to speak to you. This really isn't working for me.'

He snapped at the barista. 'A double espresso. As fast as you can. I'm running late.'

I lifted his bag onto the table. 'I've brought your things...'

'If you hang around, we could go to that new champagne bar after I finish this evening. Or would you rather just go straight for dinner? You could book a table. Text me, I'll meet you wherever.'

He was scrolling through his phone, didn't look up as he spoke. I pushed the bag a little closer.

'I thought I'd stay over again tonight; it's easier for me in the morning.'

'I've brought your things,' I repeated.

'Or you could just go home and cook, I'll join you later.'

'I won't be there. I'm meeting friends. I'd better go.'

I stood to leave, didn't look back when he called after me.

'You've left your bag on the table.'

In Hope of Bread
by Caroline Kohl

Longlisted, Scottish Arts Club Short Story Competition 2022

There is a war veteran on my kitchen floor.

He kneels on the brown linoleum and peers down the narrow gap between the oven and the end of the kitchen unit.

'I turned it on and there was a fire,' I explain, from a safe distance. 'So I turned off the electricity and rang the landlady.'

He sighs and shuffles round to address me.

'I'll pull it out and look.'

'I wanted to bake a cake.'

'Well, move and I will look.'

I shrink slightly in my slippers. I have been living in Russia for almost three months now, but I am still unaccustomed to this bluntness. My tongue trips over three-syllable pleases and thank you's as I apologise my way through a one-year Moscow secondment with the bank that will surely stand out on my CV. Nobody cares how sorry I am for standing in the wrong queue at the post office, or how enthusiastically I express my gratitude when a fellow passenger lets me squeeze down the crowded metro carriage so I can get off at my stop. They just want me to stay out of their way.

My landlady is no exception. Yelena Nikolaevna also owns the flat next door, but she is often away in the countryside and I rarely see her. She sees me, though, through the pinhole camera that she has installed next to the heavy metal door that permits entry to our communal vestibule. Her eldest son streams the footage through their TV and replays the highlights in daily phone calls to the dacha.

'I like to know we are safe,' she told me, 'And that you do not have loud parties, unlike the last foreigner who lived here.'

I wonder if asking Kirill to do the maintenance is just another way for Yelena Nikolaevna to keep tabs on me. Kirill is a short, wiry man with dark Cyrillic tattoos that punctuate his knuckles. He is at least my father's age, but I can clearly see the outline of his biceps through his neat grey t-shirt. I doubt anyone would want to cause him trouble.

'Why are you standing there, girl? Move!'

Kirill swats me into the corner of the room, somewhere in between the kitchen table and the double windows. I skid and catch myself in the thick yellow net curtain, fumbling my way out like a shy bride. If there is a way to unlearn the helplessness of being a young single woman in a strange land, I haven't found it.

To the all-important question:

'Kirill Kirillovich. Tea?'

He holds up a finger to shush me.

'Not yet. Later.'

Kirill squats low to the ground, wraps his arms around the oven, and pulls.

Once the oven is out of its corpus, the problem is clear. The plug has melted into the blackened socket and behind the oven cable, a charred trail runs down the wallpaper to the dusty floor. I gasp, glad that I switched off the mains when I did.

Kirill shrugs.

'It could be worse. I can fix this. I will go to my car.'

My first interaction with Kirill — when the not-so-secret hidden camera malfunctioned and made its presence known with an aggressive high-pitched bzzziiiiing — had taught me that there was nothing he didn't keep in the boot of his roughed-up Zhiguli. It was then that he'd mentioned the army.

'I served. Therefore I am always prepared.'

He returns with his toolbox in one hand and a new plug and socket in the other, and sets the lot down on the kitchen floor. I am trapped in the corner of the room. I briefly contemplate making my excuses and tip-toeing through his workspace to busy myself elsewhere in the flat — but it is a Saturday afternoon, the clouds are swollen with the threat of snow, and I am still new enough to the

165

city to have acquaintances rather than friends. Besides, I don't think I have enough Russian to explain myself.

I sit and watch Kirill at work, his upper body twisting awkwardly as he unscrews the remnants of the wall socket. His t-shirt rises up his back slightly, and I catch a glimpse of a mark on his skin just above the waistband of his off-brand jeans.

'Oh! What is your tattoo?' My face flushes with embarrassment. 'Er... sorry. I just saw it.'

Kirill pulls his head out from under the counter — where my flour, eggs, and sugar stand, abandoned — and looks at me.

'It's a mountain. Like the mountains in Afghanistan.'

'Did you serve there?'

'Yes. In the eighties.'

I am reaching the limits of my Russian already. It doesn't matter, Kirill is back at the wall, attaching the new socket. How long would it have taken for the fire to swallow my jumble of a kitchen? I have heard horror stories about life in these old Soviet apartment buildings — whole towers tumbling like puzzle blocks because one person knocked two rooms into one, or installed a whirlpool tub. They call it European renovation.

'Did you... like it?' I offer. He grunts.

'Did I like it? It was war! Of course I didn't like it.'

Kirill waves his hand back towards me and says something I don't understand. It takes me a moment to realize that he is gesturing for the wire cutters and the replacement plug, both of which lie at my feet. I pass them to him and bear the weight of silence, not knowing what else to say. It is snowing heavily now and the trees in the courtyard are suffocating. I think of the other times that I have seen snow come down like this, tucked up in a ski chalet with a cup of hot chocolate warm against my stomach.

Rubber feet screech along the floor. The work is done, the kitchen saved, the oven rammed back into place. I can turn on the electricity again. I stand up.

'Kirill Kirillovich. Tea?'

*

We sit at the small kitchen table with the pot between us. It is nauseatingly British — a porcelain Union Jack gifted from my office mates when I transferred to Moscow. They told me to teach teatime to the Russians. Actually, the Russians are teaching it to me. I let the leaves steep for longer than I would at home, and we offset the tea's bitterness with a spoonful of jam.

'I'm sorry I don't have cake.' I say, remembering the stalled baking experiment at the same time as I remember that Russians rarely take tea without a biscuit.

Kirill shrugs.

'It happens. Do you like to bake?'

'I like bread,' I say, not knowing how to tell him that all I'd really wanted to do that afternoon was bake a marble cake that would remind me of my mum's. How it had taken me three visits to the supermarket to work out which flour would be best. How I couldn't find the cocoa powder in the purple cardboard tub, how I'd had to buy a box with a creepy baby's face on it instead.

'I like bread too. Black bread. White bread. Naan.'

'Naan? When do you eat naan?'. Kirill looks down and stirs his tea. I am surprised. Naan is a cheeky takeaway after a late night at the office, or a noisy night out with friends on Curry Mile. It is not afternoon tea with a fifty-something Russian handyman in a disintegrating Moscow kitchen.

He looks back up at me and taps his teaspoon on the side of his cup.

'I first ate naan in the 1980s. At a wedding in Afghanistan.'

'Are you married?'

'No, I am not married. I went to Afghanistan because I was not married. It was not my wedding.'

I try to picture Kirill as a young soldier abroad, simultaneously at war and at a wedding. As in all my Russian conversations, I worry that I have misunderstood — that a consonant has slipped between my ears and I have inadvertently followed the story down the wrong path.

It is late afternoon; I get up and cross the room to turn on the light.

'I was in the mountains,' Kirill continues, under a dim glow. 'I was lost. I was alone, hungry. It was very cold. It was dangerous. Then I saw a building, so I walked to it. And found a wedding.'

I reach for the teapot and he offers up his cup for a refill. I oblige, and then watch him add more blackcurrant jam. 'I arrived, and everything stopped. All eyes were on me. Silence. I didn't know what to do.' He takes his teacup in one hand, and forms a pistol with the other. 'You know, because I am Russian. Paf paf paf!' Kirill waves his fist in the air, two fingers firing bullets in my direction. We lock eyes for a moment. 'Everyone was looking at me.

'Women, all looking at me. The only Russian. The only man.'

It will be ten years before I remember this conversation, and spend my evening reading up on the Soviet war in Afghanistan. It will be ten years before I learn about the Great Game, the mujahideen, and the Panjshir offensives. The boyish soldiers. The civilian deaths. It will be ten years before I think that this is a story about anything other than a half-baked attempt at small conversation in a language that is not my own.

Kirill Kirillovich will be gone by this time too, although I won't know it yet.

'Then the bride came. She gave me a piece of naan.' He smiled softly into his teacup. 'And that was it.'

*

I am standing at the countertop with floured hands. I scoop the dough out of the mixing bowl and thud it onto the wooden surface, driving my knuckles into its soft weight. It has been a long time since I left Moscow, and took my tea with anything other than milk and a sprinkle of sugar. My Russian linguistic abilities have withered on the vine. But I do bake: bread, not marble cake. Tonight, we're having curry, and my eldest has requested homemade naan.

I know — now — that Kirill's naan was not my naan. Naan binds Eurasia like a promise: you can trace a line from India to the UK and whichever route you take, you will find naan, or nan, or non. It is baked everywhere, in one form or another. Nan is the Persian word for bread, and I have been fortunate to break bread in many countries since my year in Russia.

I freckle the dough with poppy seeds and fold it one last time before returning it to the bowl. I cover it with a damp cloth and slot it into the airing cupboard, where it will puff proudly until I retrieve it.

It is the magical hour between the end of my work day and the start of our evening as a family. The next minutes are mine, until the children come back from their after-school clubs and my husband unlocks his bike at the railway station and cycles the final two miles home. I wish he would take the bus instead. I worry about him, cycling along busy roads alone. We are only ever one moment away from danger, aren't we?

The curry simmers on the stove and I let it fog up the kitchen window on purpose, revelling in the humidity. The radio hums in the background. Across a small sea and many mountains, troops are withdrawing from Afghanistan.

Final Rinse
by Andrew Gardiner

Shortlisted, Edinburgh Award for Flash Fiction 2022

The machines we have here are so big they'll take an Emperor. That's one up from Super King. Most duvets are carefully folded to hide the stain but there's really no need for embarrassment. We don't judge. We get all sorts. A lot of cat owners from fancy flats in Stockbridge come in. A surprising number like to pee on the bed — the cats, that is.

We know the score, which setting for which stain, all the tricks of the trade. Cold wash for blood. It's usually a nosebleed but I reckon I've washed away the evidence of a murder. We've seen it all but you need to speak to us to get the best result. We can't be shocked even if the ticket booth looks like a confessional.

When I retire, I'll miss my machines. They're a different breed from your Beckos and your Hotpoints. Most are from Germany with names you wouldn't know and keep going day in day out for years — true work horses, tens of thousands of wash cycles. They all have their quirks: different voices, how much they shake, how greedy for powder. There's one that's very sensitive to hair and oose but she does a great job with big towel loads. Yes, she.

I've never had a washing machine of my own, so that's another way I'll miss them. The ones in John Lewis look like silly wee toys. I can't take them seriously. I've never minded washing my dirty laundry in public.

Leaf
by Jane Pearn

Longlisted, Scottish Arts Club Short Story Competition 2022

Isla feels a guilty relief to be out of the house. For the past few weeks it has been her daily and necessary half hour. Pete understands her need to be in fresh air, free from the sweet, heavy smell of sickness that no open window can dispel. Free to move at a brisk pace without the fear of waking him into pain. She always waits until after the district nurse's daily visit, so she knows she's left him comfortable. She carries with her the image of his face, the shadowed eyes, skin the colour of buttermilk against the white pillow. His dark hair, grown back finer and silkier, combed. The sheet tucked tidily around him.

This walk around the loch used to be their weekend routine. There was interest in every season. In the dead of winter, silent snowflakes would feather the frozen water. Then would come the shy surprise of the first spring flowers, followed by May bluebells forming a purple haze. In June, hundreds of foxgloves, pink and mauve and white, standing tall, made a guard of honour on either side of the path up the hillside. And of course, there were the summer ducklings. She had felt a smiling responsibility to count them every time, to make sure that each ping-pong ball of fluff was growing, almost while they watched, into a capable little duck, ready to begin the cycle again. Then the rustling autumn carpet, and the urge to scuffle through that golden sweetness, which somehow carried the scent of bonfires. So many leaves, so many trees, each with their own character and distinctive shape.

Pete admired the huge sequoia, but the ancient horse chestnut is her favourite. It brushes the water with its lower branches and soars skywards. She likes to imagine its roots reaching into the soil, into the loch bed, an echo of the massive canopy above. It is a cathedral of living wood, now in its midsummer glory. She has watched it through so many seasons, she counts it as a friend. 'Tree', she calls it. Just Tree. On still days it looks back at itself from the water, so that it seems to be a hollow sphere of branches. She remembers how sometimes they would come equipped with paper and pencils. They'd sit side by side on a fallen log trying to sketch it, and ruefully failing to capture the illusion.

She thinks how strange it feels, to miss someone who is still here. A surge of anger: she doesn't want to be in these woods on her own, with memories her only company, while Pete lies in his own world, dying. She wants him beside her, to hear the weight of his tread keeping time with hers. To feel the warmth of his hand helping her over a stile. It's not his fault, of course it isn't. But she feels betrayed. Another lover is stealing his body, bit by bit. And all she can do is watch.

Sophie's been understanding, told her to take all the time she needs. But when they speak, Isla hears the strain in Sophie's voice, trying to keep their small craft business going single-handed. At first she tried to make Isla laugh with her tales of the temps and their mistakes. Now, not so much. They are both in limbo, waiting. Suddenly, Isla desperately wants to be at work, having normal conversations about ordinary things. She misses the jokes, the coffee-shop takeaways, even the shared worry when business is slow. But to admit, even to herself, that she misses them makes her feel shallow and disloyal.

The woods are loud with birdsong today. There are a thousand greens, studded with bright splashes of buttercup and red campion, herb robert and wild geraniums. She strides on, letting the rhythmic crunch of her footfalls on the gravel form a backdrop to her thoughts. Thoughts that seep into her mind like floodwater under a door. Sooner than she expects she reaches the chestnut, intending to give it her usual brief stroke. She tries to move on but finds herself rooted to the path. Tree has something to say. There are eyes in the deep scored bark and they are looking not at her, but into her. A breeze stirs the leaves. Tree shakes its head. It whispers, 'I know what you're thinking.'

There'd be no need for pressure on the pillow, just the weight of it would be enough. Then stillness, release, peace. He'd wanted to come home and she'd agreed, wanting him to be with her, where he belonged. They'd accepted, both of them, that he would die but they hadn't known — nobody knew — how long it would take.

Isla wants it to be over and she dreads it being over. He'd always said, hadn't he — *if it gets too much.* Too much for him? Or too much for her? Day after day, night after wracking night, he in the ugly borrowed hospital bed in their pretty sitting room, now cluttered with the paraphernalia of illness — the array of bottles, the boxes of pills, the drip stand. She pottering quietly in the kitchen, making meals that are now just for her, or reading to him, or dozing uncomfortably in the armchair. The shelves are crowded with photos, in cheap frames or just propped up and starting to curl. When he'd come home from the hospice, he'd asked her to print them out, and surround him with them. Now, she doesn't think he notices. Photos of them climbing, sailing, laughing, squinting into the sun. They'd thought they had all the time in the world — and why wouldn't they? The thought jolts her again: they will make no more new memories together, ever.

It had always been just the two of them. She wonders if children might have been a comfort — would they be a source of strength, or have needs she couldn't meet, grief she couldn't heal? Too late. It was the road not travelled.

She remembers seeing Pete off on a train last year. Last year? Really? It felt, at the same time, like yesterday and like a different, impossibly distant life. They'd said their goodbyes, but the train's departure was delayed and she'd lingered awkwardly on the platform. He'd laughingly waved her away, mouthing through the glass,

'Go, just go!'

In the end, she'd moved away, conscious of his eyes on her back. She'd turned every few steps to wave even when she couldn't make out his face. As she left the station concourse she'd looked over her shoulder one more time, to see an empty grey platform. And she'd felt an unexpected ache in her throat.

He is withdrawing to a distant land. He must make the journey alone, and this time she can't turn away. But it's hard to keep waving goodbye.

When he is awake, she sees him watching clouds framed by the window, drifting as he too is drifting. At these moments he seems to be floating away. And then he comes back. She feels relief with a twinge of disappointment. She hates herself for the twinge but can't control it. Tree says, 'I know. You're not the first.'

Last night's wind has torn away some leaves. She bends down to select the best, chooses one with five evenly spaced leaflets, still a vivid emerald. 'There are seasons,' says Tree. She carefully rolls up the leaf and slides it into the pocket of her jacket. From far off comes a growl of thunder. The light changes and the sky turns dull pewter. The birds have fallen silent. A shiver of raindrops reaches her bare head. It's time to go home.

She turns the door handle quietly. That cloying smell, that sense of time suspended. He barely makes a shape under the covers, and he seems too still to be asleep. Isla is holding her breath. He makes a sound and she exhales, tears quivering on her breath. He opens his eyes wide in a spasm of pain, but he manages a small smile and raises an eyebrow in query.

'Yes,' she says, 'Tree is looking grand. It sends its love.'

His eyes are closed again but his fists are clenched. She feels in her pocket and takes out the leaf. First she places it like a cool green hand over his face.

The Crinkle and the Crumb
by Julie Dron

Commendation, Edinburgh Award for Flash Fiction 2022

She tugs the sheet, a crease appears at the opposite end of the mattress. Minutes wasted, back and forth; straighten, pucker, pull, crinkle. Rita fantasizes, gnashing her teeth and shredding the sheet, the bed, the house; compromises and covers a stubborn crinkle with quilt and pillows. Walking downstairs, not touching the polished banister, reciting her mantra, 'one crease doth not a failure make'. Further distress discovering a cup carelessly placed on shelf disrupting her careful colour coordination. Cleaning invisible oily fingerprints from cupboard doors.

Fifteen minutes till noon, tea and buttered toast with Leah in Le Bistro. No longer buttering toast in her kitchen because the pain far exceeds the pleasure. Crumbs collecting in bread bin corners, falling silently like midnight snow, onto worktops, tables, her clothes, the floor. Toasted black and brown, crispy crumbs begetting more crumbs and so on ad infinitum culminating in Jackson Pollock sink; water splashing, swirling, splattering crumbs stuck to basin sides. Wiping surfaces, hoovering, sucking up crumbs not visible to the naked eye.

Ten minutes. Clenching and unclenching fingers, digging nails into palms, the image of the crinkled sheet pounding, pounding, louder, louder. Nine minutes. She succumbs, races upstairs, pulls away the quilt and pillows, slides the heated iron over the sheet. Exhaling long breaths of relief like the nicotine addict whose cigarette brings temporary comfort. Exhausted, surveying the streamlined perfection with a deep yearning to float into the pure whiteness; no sight, no sound, no being, no dust.

Condition: *Spinster*
by Michael Toolan

Longlisted, Scottish Arts Club Short Story Competition 2022

Afterwards, she wheels the bike to Flannery's and buys tea, sugar, Indian meal, and a bar of Cadbury's chocolate for the children to share. She had thought of going to say a prayer at the Cathedral, or seeing if Norah was at home — she would have loved a talk with her sister — but she had to get back. She knew James would be frazzled, between the children and all the neighbours calling in and needing to say their piece and sit and sympathise.

*

The ride in had been lovely, even with the rainshower that passed over just as she reached the macadamed road that stretched away to Carracastle where they had burned the police barracks at the weekend. You could still smell it in the air, different altogether from that of burning turf: acrid, brutal, maybe wicked even. She cycled the other way, into Ballagh' — half an hour spinning along in the fresh air, loving the feel of her legs pumping and her lungs full, flying along as if she had no cares. A bike ride was still enough of a novelty to be thrilling, the easy smoothness of it and the speed, after the jolting motion on cart or horseback. There were few other riders on the road, and not a single motor car. The only horse and trap she passed was old Jimmy Morrisroe, who by the looks of it was fetching a pile of big stones from the old lands. Best of all it was half an hour that took her mind off the grieving by showing the beauty in the world. Especially the fragrance of the new grass rising in the fields, a dazzling green against the enclosing stone walls shining from the rain. And then the calves and lambs all in together, careering and frolicking in those fields, while their mothers sat unconcerned, ruminating. The young looked so healthy, every last one; they must have only dropped in the past day or two. Down a lane here and there, or further away seemingly surrounded by fields, the whitewashed cottages sparkled in the sun whenever the clouds moved on. Each front door was wide open, and most had a gently smoking chimney poking above the thatched roof: a pretty picture, seen at this distance at least. And all of it — the cottages, the fields, the animals — belonged now to her neighbours: Toweys, Dooneys, Costellos and Quinns. That made her proud and some way content, whatever came out of the skirmishes between the British soldiers and the lads burning the barracks and looking for policemen to shoot or weapons to lift.

It was because of all the unrest that Bridget had insisted on being the one to go into town. Patrick was her husband's father, not hers, so on that score James might better have been the one to do the reporting. And besides the visitors coming and going there were the children to keep an eye on (especially the eldest, Margaret, sickly again), off school because of Easter. All of that would be Bridget's work usually. But because of the disturbances — the war, as they called it in Dublin — Bridget was adamant that James stayed on the farm. She wanted him well away from any trouble. She knew, or heard from others in the townland, how easily a bit of talk could get out of hand. The next thing you knew some harmless neighbour had become the target of a whispered boycott or been forced into joining the Brotherhood. Or had the stock of some cockney Tan's rifle break his jaw, for looking at him the wrong way or not saying Sir. The savages, she thought, hadn't they seen and done enough killing in France? Or had it made them fit for nothing else? 'Bloodlust' she'd seen it called. No, she told him: he wasn't some callow youth now, without a care in the world, free to die for Ireland. He was thirty-nine with a wife and children — at this last word a pang went through her — a wife and children that he was responsible for, and she forbade it!

Her shoulders were heaving with the deep sighs of grief racking her chest, and he went to her and held her in his arms until she calmed. It was her distress more than any argument that made him relent.

177

'Let you go then, so' he said, and went out to check on the cattle before she left the house.

*

She pedalled down Main Street to the bottom, rested her bike against the railings outside the police station, and went into the Registry office next door. It was just Anne O'Connell at the front desk, a kind soul, always discreet about other people's business, whether joy or sorrow. Anne knocked on the smoked glass door to the inner office and out came John Davey. It was a comfort that it was John, and not the Superintendent, Flanagan, on one of his visits from Castlerea — a cold fish, probably not travelling around the district much at present, avoiding attention. Bridget knew John well, had been at school with his sister Eileen. She would have asked after her but now was not the time.

'I need to register a death, John.'

'Right so.'

'It's my husband's father, Patrick Vesey. He died last Friday, Good Friday.'

'Well I'm sorry to hear that, Bridget. Please accept my condolences to yourself and James and the family.'

'Thank you.'

'Last Friday, the Second of April then.'

'Yes.'

He refrained from remarking it was a good holy day to go to one's Maker. The less said the better when dealing with the bereaved, he had learned.

He brought up the appropriate register from under the counter and opened it at the current, half-filled page. Then he slid it along the counter out of the way.

'If you don't mind, I'll just go through the details with you first, before I put anything into the register.'

'Very good,' she says. She would have done the same herself.

Unscrewing his fountain pen he asked Bridget for the information required, putting it down with some care on a sheet of scrap paper. First, the date and place of death, then the name of the deceased.

'And what was his age, at his last birthday?'

'Eighty.'

'A good long life,' John ventured, and Bridget nodded. She thought of how the old man had welcomed her into what had formerly been his house but now belonged to James and herself. He had delighted in the arrival of each new grandchild, especially when they reached two or three and became talkative and playful. Margaret first, then the others in turn down to Kathleen. Only with Bridget Veronica, born just a year ago, had he been too tired and confused to take much interest.

John Davey pressed on.

'For the deceased's rank or occupation can I put farmer?'

'You can.'

'And the cause of death?'

They briefly considered what to put, since as usual, no doctor was present at the death. They agreed on 'senile decay', as preferable to 'old age', the formula some Assistant Registrars used.

'Now what should I put under Condition?'

'Condition? Well, as I was saying, he—'

'Sorry, Bridget. It's a strange heading alright. What they want to know is was he married or widowed or single...'

'Oh!'

'Well obviously he was married, but is his wife still living?'

'No, she died a good while ago.'

Bridget thought fleetingly of James's mother, who died a few months before they married, her health already beginning to fail when they began courting. Bridget knew she had lived through hard years. Bitter-cold winters and sodden fields, bad harvests, low prices at market, sometimes so little food that they went to bed hungry. Still she had raised nine healthy children, bright and able, that anyone would be proud of. Except then she had to watch all but one of them leave home, never to return. Was she already travelling the same path herself, she wondered? Were she and James raising their children only to see them forced to leave, in search of decent jobs, a decent life?

'Then we'll put Widower as his Condition,' John said.

He turned around his page of notes so Bridget could read them, and went through them with her, pointing at each item in turn with the barrel of the pen, ensuring she was satisfied that all was correct. Then he concentrated on writing everything out again in the register, in his best hand.

He asked about the funeral, more out of courtesy than interest, judging their business to be at an end. He began saying something about Eileen while he reached over to grasp the leather-bound front cover and the earlier filled pages of the register, to bring it closed.

'Aah...'

'What?'

'Before you put the register away, John...'

'What is it?'

'I have another...'

Her throat is suddenly constricted and she can't get the words out. Her face is blotchy with pink patches on cheeks and forehead. A gasp of immeasurable despair escapes her. From her coat pocket she takes out a handkerchief to dab her eyes.

'Would you like to come into the office, Bridget, and sit down a while?'

'No. I'll be alright in a minute.'

*

Drawing on a tact that has become second nature in his job, he busies himself inspecting the desk below the counter; he finds it empty enough save for the other two ledgers. At the table behind him Anne O'Connell is thumping away on the office Underwood, typing up a letter that must go to the Customs House tonight. It provides a breakdown of births and deaths in the district for the first quarter of the year. The slow but steady clacking of the keys, the periodic ding and zip of the carriage return, are a welcome deflection from the silence. On a new sheet of scrap paper he once again notes down the details and checks them over carefully with her, ('Yes,' Bridget confirms, 'that is the name'). Then he writes them into the register in permanent black ink and for all time, immediately below the entry for her grandfather: Bridget Veronica, one year old at last birthday. Occupation: farmer's child, on 29th March, after one day of acute bronchitis, no medical attendant. Condition: Spinster.

John Davey watched Bridget Vesey slowly wheel her bicycle back towards the centre of town. Her head was down, as if she wanted to avoid having to talk to anyone she might know — so different from most of the country folk come into town on an errand, eager to see acquaintances, hungry for news of any kind. She had given him no indication she had the little girl's death to report as well, so now the register was out of chronological order, the old man's death recorded first when it had occurred four days later. Ach, it didn't trouble him, and Flanagan could take a running jump if he was unhappy about it. You only had to look at her, the grieving mother, to see why she wanted to hold on to her daughter that little bit longer.

Returning
by Jane Broughton

Shortlisted, Edinburgh Award for Flash Fiction 2022

The bus stopping jolted Sarah from her thoughts. She shouldered through the obstructing huddle of passengers onto the street. It was a relief to be out of that sea of strangers. She lengthened her stride, enjoying the stretch of her muscles and the crisp air.

She became aware of shouting behind her but couldn't make out words. Glancing back she noticed a man, buzz cut, huge grey overcoat, gesturing to her. He moved towards her.

Suddenly sucked back in time she whimpered, quickened her pace, stumbled, and then lurched into a full-scale pelt for home. Bruises had faded but her body remembered. Stranger/danger, stranger/danger, her feet pounded out the rhythm as she ran.

Then, gasping for breath, she was there, her glossy red gate, her solid front door, her sliding key. She crumbled behind the barricade and shuddered with each knock against her spine.

A few words, perhaps an explanation, perhaps an apology, and then her purse flopped through the letterbox like a returning salmon.

Achill
by Chris Lee

Longlisted, Scottish Arts Club Short Story Competition 2022

Sorcha walks with me on the beach at Dugort. The clouds come and go from the top of Slievemore, revealing cliffs that sheer off below the summit, treacherous in the mist. The weather system of Achill swirls and moans; it is sometimes playful, sometimes spiteful, letting intense shafts of golden light pierce through the gloom, only to be snatched away again by brooding clouds. We stroll upon the beach pretending we are natives, well worn by the teasing winds, not the Dublin blow-ins that we really are, colonising Achill with our hopeless artistic pretentions.

Sorcha has been my companion now for thirty years. I am underserving, but so are we all, undeserving of the beautiful accident that settles on some lives and passes others by totally. Sorcha's love for me is hard to understand for I have not been an easy partner to live with. But my love for her is simple; a gratitude that is occasionally magnificent in its completeness. I can manage only a few minutes of putting one foot in front of the other. I bask in the soothing glow of her patience and know how much it hurts her to see me so diminished. Yet what are you supposed to do when you're dying? Do you insist on the release of your lover, usher them away from your hearth in a great tantrum of rejection because you cannot bear their suffering at your suffering? Or do you greedily lap up their pity and their duty, ignoring the slow corrosion of love that inevitably follows the savage encumbrance of disease? Well, obviously you do neither, and obviously you do both.

It's cancer of the oesophagus. I am weakened but not yet in unbearable agony. Years of too much wine mostly. But I can still talk, I can still walk and I can hold Sorcha's hand as we share the bleak beauty of this magical island.

There's something about the light, oh but there is. We live just up there, at the top of the hill. We have built our fortress and can spy invaders coming for miles. Sheltered by the mountain, we are impregnable. Not that anyone wants to attack us. Apart from the odd critic that is. We are safe in our grand design. It was Sorcha's idea of course. She's a sculptor and I'm a painter, or I was until death grabbed me by the throat. She builds things, why not a house?

And so, it was; our studio and living space, our love nest and bucolic retreat. We work well in the same place, talking back and forth as we try to hew something from the ancient power of this site. Mostly now I just sit and mutter at Sorcha as she shapes her objects and gives them life.

I love to watch her as she works, and it is hard to imagine this ceremony of artistic confidence taking place anywhere else but here. We wondered at first if our presence on the island might be resented, especially by those who have made only a half living from the land and those who must pander to the growing tourist trade in order to remain close to their place of birth.

We were wrong. We were not resented and there is a deep community here of slightly alternative souls. We're as west as you get, still bridged to the mainland, where the wild waves and the harsh skies beckon the artist.

I am a painter. No, I must keep correcting myself, was a painter, in a semi-figurative style that I hauled up out of the depths of me. It took me years to develop. But I blossomed late to produce a body of almost passable work, of which I am sometimes almost proud. Portraits and landscapes in the browns, greys and yellows of Achill, distorted and contorted to meld with the peaty earth and the labile sky. Paint the truth by representing the soiled agony of life, weathered and misshapen by the elements of experience. 'Humdrum deformity', wrote one critic. 'Infantile ductility', said another. And yet, 'sombre mining of the essence of pain', claimed critic number three, while number four went so far as 'poet laureate of Irish damnation.'

The way you look at the world around you is changed by living on Achill. Out here there are seasons, not the vague temperature changes that Dublin thinks winter and spring are all about. Here you notice, are forced to notice, the way the land moves through the year, responds and reacts to the constant ebb and flow of the climate. There's a patience that's demanded of you. Time will simply move here at its own pace and it won't be consulting you about it. Achill teaches you to wait. And while you're waiting, you look.

I press Sorcha against me as we stop and drink in the stillness and the soft whispering water that splashes on the sand. 'What riches', I say to Sorcha. 'At least I have known this, at least I have known you.' She doesn't like my descent into sentiment.

'Just because you're dying', she tells me, 'Doesn't mean you should succumb to self-pity.'

'Oh, you cold heartless bitch', I say, and kiss her full on her lovely mouth.

It is time to tackle the hill that leads away from the beach towards our home. I know and revere every step of the way, even as my body struggles with the slope. We pass the Strand Hotel, quiet in the off-season, then a batch of white holiday cottages and behind them some real farmhouses. We move on past the long road to St Thomas', the Church of Ireland house of worship, whose gate is open in preparation for a funeral, or perhaps a wedding, or even a Christening. The old mission house appears to our right as we climb the hill; what a shameful episode, the attempt to convert the Irish peasantry as they starved to death during the Famine. Bitter memories, the viciousness of history, all that in Achill as well, not just the pretty face of the present. On we go. Our beautiful house stands glinting in the flickering light. Is it wrong to be so proud of a building, of a possession? Our haven and nest, our lookout, our hideaway. This is where we've nurtured love as well as art after all. Welcoming friends, dancing together in the wine dark evenings, touching the sky, hearts full of giddy excitement at a new picture or a new sculpture. Here we survey the north and the south coasts, the great pool of Keel Lough, and the wild grey blast of Keel Strand. Here we reside until the end, though I can hear his nibs 'the end' scrabbling around outside the door sometimes at night, when I lie awake in pain and I must admit, a little dread.

I think of the island and I resolve firmly that I will not leave this place again. Sorcha knows there's little point in anymore trips to the hospital. 'How am I doing doctor?' 'Still dying.' What started as a difficulty swallowing and constant acid reflux, is now the angel of death, squatting in my gullet. I cough and splutter with blood and mucus. Sometimes I am dizzy with the pain. Eventually there'll be no more walks, no more slow drives round Achill, and I'll be confined to my bed; all my thoughts and memories filtered by increasing doses of morphine. But we're not there yet. I can still use my eyes and shamble about carefully. I can still speak, albeit with a croak.

I have a little lie down and Sorcha works. I doze off easily enough and my memories and deepest thoughts get wonderfully scrambled with the trivial and the irritating. When I wake up, I am bewildered by what's been going on in my head. A great reckoning it's not. I am unable to put my mental house in order. When death arrives, I won't be ready. I must give Sorcha time to get her work done, I can't be bothering her with my childish needs every five minutes. She knows though, she can sense it when I'm awake again and eager to be off on our next adventure.

This afternoon we take the car down to Achill Sound, capital of our island state, and fill her up. This is the business district, with the biggest supermarket and hotels aplenty. This is where the bridge takes you back onto the mainland and the various roads to Castlebar, Westport and beyond. But we're not stopping, we're well supplied at home and we don't want to waste the hours shopping. Sorcha takes care of that; Sorcha takes care of everything. She manages to conceal the essential chores of life with her skill and creates time just for us. I know it is taking its toll, I can see the clouds of sorrow in her pearl grey eyes, but as I reach to disperse them, I understand that I cannot. I'd be best just to attend to the task in hand. We are on a journey, a small one to be sure, but there are still a thousand undiscovered countries here.

We drive slowly. Other cars can pass us by as they rush to get somewhere important, but we have nowhere special to go, and so everywhere we do go is special. I mention this to Sorcha and she stops the car. 'I want bitterness and cynicism to the end,' she tells me. 'No deathbed conversions, no weeping over lost friends or unfulfilled ambitions.' She tells me that Achill is a good place to die in if only because the scenery is so unforgiving. There's no lush, plush, soft, dewy nonsense here, just rock and water and the odd sheep.

Indeed, the craggy, battered, rockfaces of the west of the island feed our appetite for the wild and spectacular. Careless drivers have plunged to their deaths here, in the high winds. There's a fabulous savagery, even houses would be blasted into submission by the force of the weather on this road. Why do we love it so, this sturm und drang of the Atlantic, with a steely sun shattering into the waves, scattering the hard light, stirring the turmoil? We could watch this scene for hours, oblivious to the rest of the world which seems facile to us here, crammed with petty irrelevance. We hold each other, though the car is warm, while the view is piercing with its cold delight.

I feel a sharp stab of pain in my chest and then another. The intensity increases, and I gasp for air. 'The pain,' I say, 'the pain has come.' Sorcha knows what this means. I am descending, not long to go now, perhaps I'm saying goodbye to the waves for the last time. The pain gets worse with every metre we travel but even the pain gets exhausted with the effort and it eases off by the time I'm propped up in bed. I laugh and tell Sorcha that we should go back to the cliffs because the pain has lost its grip. She pours me a glass of red wine, and I sip the poison that has helped to kill me. My, it tastes good. Years of self-neglect have led to this moment. I am abandoning my lover because I failed to keep myself healthy. What a fool, what a churl. I tell her I'm sorry once again, but she just refills my glass and shrugs. I make my familiar excuses.

'Ah well, you have the house and a pile of mediocre paintings to remember me by.'

'It'll take a fair while to flog those off.'

'You'll be glad of the space when I'm not under your feet.'

'You're not dead yet, there's at least half a bottle to go.'

'I'll drink to that.'

Sorcha wipes away a silent tear.

'Let's just watch the light.'

And so, we do.

Wormhole
by Etienne Essery

Shortlisted, Edinburgh Award for Flash Fiction 2022

Dylan found the hole and lay face down on the dry brown crust of grass that carpeted the playground. The stiff woody bristles pricked his skin and a long one went up his nose, scraping the delicate membrane inside. Recoiling, Dylan could taste and smell the salty blood as it trickled out his nose and down the back of his throat.

'You been fighting?' the teacher asked. 'Look at this shirt — your ma's gonna skin you...' Catching herself, the young teacher put her arm around the boy, remembering that his mother had passed away that summer. 'Sorry love, I know it must be hard,' she whispered, before he pulled away.

What did she know — not to be able to talk to Mother, to say sorry and beg forgiveness. Peering once more down the volcano-rimmed hole Dylan recalled the words, the ones that killed her:

'You're so ugly; I wish you would go away!' he'd said, angry with her for denying him the ice cream. The fact that the conversation happened months before she died, and that they'd made up and hugged that very afternoon, meant nothing — he would forever be held in thrall by the sentence he'd once issued and recently remembered.

But maybe there was a way, after all: the space program he'd watched on TV said that wormholes in the cosmos could connect him to the past, and although Dylan knew it was a bit different, talking down the hole in the parched earth comforted him.

The Last Puppet
by Catherine Ogston

Longlisted, Scottish Arts Club Short Story Competition 2022

Magnus was a puppet maker; he carved slender wooden limbs that swayed and softly click-clacked together, and then strung them together with fine cord until they could perform graceful movements. I liked to watch his face, deep in concentration, and his hands moving like an artist's, conjuring something beautiful from blocks of rough wood.

In daylight his line of puppets looked harmless, their arms and legs elegantly shaped and lying slack, their heads egg-shaped ovals waiting for paint and decoration. But in the dark they looked macabre — a procession of demon dolls ready to come to life and perform a tormented dance. I refused to go into his workshop after dark, scared of what I might see and the spell they might cast on me.

'Catriona, there are enough trows and spirits on Yell, you do not need to be worrying about my harmless wooden puppets hanging in the shed,' he would tell me. It was in our blood to believe in the northern fairies and elves, many of them troublesome and thieves. But although these were tales from our childhood it seemed my mind had not left them behind. Something must have bothered our spaniel Hamish also, as he would lie on the mat at the back door and not budge.

'The dog agrees with me,' I would say and Magnus would only answer that Hamish was lazy and too fond of the heat of the kitchen aga. Still I wouldn't go to the workshop once the sun had dipped under the horizon, which in winter-time happened as early as three in the afternoon. From time to time Magnus would ask me to walk across the garden to his workshop to fetch something he had left behind and I would tell him no, I would not set foot inside while all those dolls lay in wait for me, shrouded by shadows.

'They'll no bite!' he would laugh and that only summoned thoughts of puppets lunging at me with their smooth faceless heads, sharp pointed teeth appearing as they gnawed into my skin. He knew my over-active thoughts and he laughed gently at me, and I let him because I knew it was all my own ridiculousness. Besides, those puppets paid half our bills and I had to put up with them whether I liked them or not.

Magnus came from a long line of shipbuilders but he did not breathe in the salt of sea air as he cut and planed timber or feel his muscles burn as he shaped and nailed planks. However wood dust settled in his lungs just the same. It was amid the days of endless summer sunlight when he went to see the doctor. The diagnosis came after weeks of tests and scans and trips to the mainland. Lung disease and a poor prognosis. He was gone before the winter darkness fell upon the land again.

*

I left the workshop untouched for two weeks after the funeral. Then I logged into the business account and read the emails waiting for orders to be fulfilled. I unlocked the door and swung it open, suspicious of the puppets' activities, having been left idle for so long. But they were hanging in orderly queues as if they were obedient pets waiting for their master's return. Weak winter light streamed in from outside, a strong sea wind blowing, and I could see every speck of the sawdust strewn benches and the rack of tools. Hamish sat at my feet as I lifted the first puppet down and felt its heavy weight in my hands. My fingers tingled as I realised the last hands to hold this belonged to Magnus, my husband who now was lying in the church graveyard with his ancestors. I spent a long moment like that before I wrapped that puppet and sent it away, the address label somewhere I had never heard of and didn't care about because my life was here on my island, even though it was now a half-life, cleaved in two and diminished. Magnus hadn't even reached fifty.

I carried on like that, packing each puppet and sending it away until the order book was empty. Then all that remained was one complete puppet and an assortment of random legs and arms, a few rolling heads. I swept the leftover limbs into a box and put it high on a shelf. The remaining puppet and I confronted each other, its face unseeing and emotionless; mine filled with too much emotion. Perhaps I felt sorry for it, left on its own, abandoned and solitary. Eventually I spoke aloud to it. 'You're coming with me,' I said, 'so long as you behave yourself.'

Hamish lifted his head and cocked his ears. Then he whined softly but he did not protest as I locked the workshop door and the three of us went inside the house. I hung the puppet on a hook where Magnus had always hung his cap. I had given it away to his best friend and the hook seemed too empty, bereft of any useful purpose. For the first thirty or so times that I walked past it the puppet seemed to catch my suspicious eye, and then I grew used to it and it became part of the wall, part of the house, part of my life I was trying to rebuild without Magnus.

Two winter moons passed without disturbance to my days. I worked and walked with Hamish, laid flowers in the graveyard and tried to tell myself that things would not always feel so bleak. Hamish would lick my hand and lay his head in my arms as if to give me encouragement; I thanked him every day for his companionship and his acceptance that our lives were so dull and flat and without joy.

It was the end of February when I had a nightmare. In my dream I was inside my house which was surrounded by the shadows of hideous creatures creeping around and trying to enter. They were small in stature with short bodies and long limbs and had fast quick movements, badness reeking from them as they cackled at my fear. I woke in a cold sweat to find Hamish panting beside my bed.

The bad dreams continued, coming every third night or so. I cut out caffeine and late-night television, I had calming baths and drank herbal tea but nothing worked. The creatures — in my bones I knew them to be trows, the elves of folktales who stoles islanders' cows, fresh milk and brides and babies — continued their wicked dance around my house, terrorising me. After the fifth dream the noise of knocking woke me. It consisted of loud click-clack sounds, like wood against stone. My heart yammering, I crept out of bed and peered out the bedroom door. A draught gusted through a window I had not remembered opening so I heaved it shut and surveyed the house. Everything was still. The puppet's feet were motionless against the wall. Calming myself I climbed back into bed, everything outside quiet in the glow of the cold moonlight. It was only as I lay quietly willing sleep to overtake me again that I realised that Hamish was panting in an irregular anguished way.

I ran my fingers over his small body trying to find the source of his pain. It did not take me long; wedged into his side was a long splinter of wood. I pulled it out and held it in my palm. Hamish licked his wound as I stared at the arrow shaped shard. Elf-shot. That was what it had been called when islanders' animals were attacked by the trows; pierced with a sharp trow-made and trow-fired weapon. Tiptoeing to the hall I stared at the puppet's face, its blank head lolling against the wall. With a deep breath I touched it, allowing my fingers to test for smoothness on each part of its torso and limbs. And there, on the back of one leg, there was a needle-sharp twinge to my fingertip, where wood had been roughly prised out. Lifting it into the light of the full moon, I saw a splinter shaped strip missing from the wood.

I did not sleep a wink after that. As the hours of darkness rolled towards the dawn I pulled old books from the bookcase and read the ancient stories of hill trows, trolls and peerie folk. There was nothing about bewitched puppets. But as day broke Hamish and I were standing on the cliff's edge, the box from the workshop in my hands and the puppet at my feet. I could hardly bring myself to touch it, perhaps in case it burned my skin or came to life in my hands. The sea crashed onto the rocks below, a swirling cauldron, and I stared down into it, readying myself to throw the last of Magnus' work into the abyss.

Except that's what was holding me back. How could objects carved and created by a gentle person, a person who loved me without hesitation or judgement, be responsible for hurting me or Hamish? I had to be certain before I threw the contents down into the crashing waves.

Were the trows to blame? They had seemed so real and life-like, flitting around outside my windows, letting their shadows grow into monstrous giants in my dreams. Had they fashioned the arrow from the wooden leg of the puppet to fire towards me? And why? What business did the trows have with me? I had nothing they could want or need.

But even as I thought those words my mind was counting dates, and adding days and weeks in rough calculations. As the sun started its slow brief progress across the sky I was walking back into the house with Hamish at my feet and the box under my arm, the puppet and the wooden pieces softly bumping into each other.

*

The nursery was complete a month before the baby was due. I made the cradle myself from planks of wood in the workshop, and with help from friends and a few manuals and late-night internet investigations. The puppet hangs on the wall facing the sea-view. One day I might make clothes for it, or adorn it in some way but for now I am content that it is just as Magnus fashioned it. I have sanded down the place where the splinter had been gouged from. I didn't need a reminder of that.

Around my neck I wear a necklace of cord and the elf-arrow as a pendant. The stories tell that any human who has possession of one is immune from hurt and protected from further trouble by the trows and so it stays with me always.

Sometimes as I close the door I hear a tiny sound, a minute wooden foot knocking against the wall. I never see anything and the sound is so faint that perhaps I imagine it. But I like to think it is Magnus' way of telling me he is still with us both.

Why they like to lie
by Ros Thomas

Longlisted, Edinburgh Award for Flash Fiction 2022

People stop lying to you when you're dying. But you need proof: you're laid out on a gurney breathing hospital fug. A drip's in your arm. Possibly morphine, but pethidine will do, if Death is coming soon. Like Friday.

'Prognosis terminal,' Dr Ahmadi says. 'From the stroke or the drink. The head injury doesn't help.'

If you're really dying, you'll get the lowdown on family mysteries. Like why Grandma took a shine to voodoo after Grandpa took a shine to that Cuban cleaning lady. Or why Uncle Morrie never married and always holidayed in Pattaya.

Time relaxes when you're dying. At least for other people. They'll sit beside you for hours. You become a confessional. 'Pull the curtain nurse? Now, darling, I've never forgiven myself for sleeping with Gordon. I guess it was payback for... never mind.'

Death arrives late. On Sunday.

Your moist-eyed friends mill about at your funeral.

'So the stroke got him?'

'Well, the cork got him first.'

'Cork?'

'Didn't you hear? Popped himself in the head. Then had a stroke.'

Gasps.

'Poor Margo.'

At your wake, the truth about your drinking seeps out as the grog soaks in. Margot starts on your failed attempts at A.A, your droopy pecker and that fraud squad inquiry. Now you're glad you're gone.

Death's truths are brutal: 'Margot's moved in with Gordon.'

'Already?'

'She binned your stuff.'
'Even my watercolours?'
'No. She burnt those.'
Death will amuse himself for weeks with your demise.
Mort By Cork.
He's good at epitaphs.

Down with the Doubles
by Lorraine Queen

Longlisted, Edinburgh Award for Flash Fiction 2022

Long strands of greasy hair brushed the sticky, wet table. His muttering reverberated in the empty bar.

He lifted his head and tried to focus. 'Frankie! Gie's another large wan.'

'It's no table service Harry.'

Harry's head slumped and he began to hum in a low phlegmy voice. The door opened and in walked a thin woman holding her coat tightly around her.

'He came in at three, an' he's been on doubles a' day Liz.'

She nodded and said, 'Ah'll see if ah can get him up the road Frankie. Harry! Harry 'mon. Time to go, let's get you hame.'

Harry looked up at the sound of her voice. 'Hame? Naw Liz it's too lonely withoot her. Jist leave me.' Then he began to sing, 'When I was a lad and Shep was a pup...'

The barman acted swiftly. 'Aw naw Harry. Ah've nae entertainment licence. D'ye want tae get me shut doon?'

Stumbling to the door, Harry burrowed into the fur of his sister's coat, wiping his tears and snot in a single movement.

Liz turned to the barman. 'He fair misses her, but no' as much as he misses the extra dosh. Wisnae many could resist that wee dug lookin' up while he sang in Buchanan Street?'

'Aye, he's grievin' hard so he is.'

'Grievin' hard? Three weeks he's been like this. When oor mither died the bastard was up at the dancin' straight from the fuckin' undertakers!'

And they stumbled into the grey Glasgow night.

Gulag
by Orla Murphy

Longlisted, Scottish Arts Club Short Story Competition 2022

Anastasia looked out onto her garden and saw the white grass and barren flower beds that were framed by the diluted winter light. The top of the wall sparkled, varnished with frost. The stove had started to release its limp wisps of heat but the chill was no matter. She had been much, much colder. The Committee would receive her at 2pm. The state bus departed just after 9am. It would stop near Committee HQ where the appointed administrator would meet her. Pushkin stretched and yawned and tucked his tail beneath him to sleep again, his orange coat blazing against the old, checked throw.

She washed quickly and dressed. A plaid skirt. Thick tan stockings. A burgundy jumper and blouse. Her good brown shoes looked a little dull, but they would suffice.

At 8:58am she walked purposefully to the bus stop. The path in the shade was slick with frost and ice, but it wouldn't slow her. Citizens averted their eyes on her approach. She coexisted with them, on the perimeter, which suited both.

The state bus was full and damp. A stranger with a huge beard and a Cossack's hat smiled at her, but she stared through him, to the fields — frosted and endless. Forty summers ago, she watched the darting of insects and field mice below her while lying on bales in fields like these; unseen because her overall was the colour of straw. Hiding from the overseer and daring the sunlight to expose her presence. It never did, even when they were two.

Some young girls on the bus laughed and squealed loudly — about boys. The frivolity of girls still irked her. She closed her eyes and their noise faded.

At the meeting spot the young administrator smiled, offered her hand, and introduced herself as Anya. Anastasia didn't take her hand, but nodded and replied 'Anastasia.'

The administrator led the way, chattering. Was Anastasia well? Was she nervous? Assuring that there was no need for nerves as this was just a process that had to be undertaken. Anastasia mentally assigned the steps up to the large building to decades, to focus her mind.

Step 1–1963–the end and the beginning. Step 2–1973–the middle. Step 3–1983–the beginning and the end. Step 4–1993–the adjustment. Step 5–2003–the settling. Step 6–yet to be concluded.

The administrator met a colleague at central reception and was directed to a room where they sat. The administrator opened her file and started to go through the contents. Birth, childhood address, the family composition and the occupation of father (tenant farmer) and mother (wife/mother) were confirmed. The younger woman asked, 'Were there any mental deficiencies in the family?' Anastasia replied that there was the uncle who drank spirits endlessly and the mother who was tormented with her nerves; both were dead.

The administrator shifted uneasily. Was she schooled?

'Yes, until 13 years, then the farm.'

Was she literate?

'Yes.'

The administrator wondered, did she write well?

'Well enough; I wrote half of that,' Anastasia said, pointing to the file. The younger woman flushed.

The administrator said there were six Committee members and they would sit at a top table. They were chosen by Government. One *even* represented the President. *Very important*, she stressed. Anastasia had one question, 'How many women?'

One, it seemed.

The administrator said that would describe Anastasia's life before Gulag and in Gulag, but they would ask questions, and she must answer. She simply must she said, firmly. Anastasia knew that

199

this administrator had a role to fulfil and had drawn a short straw today. She also knew that she wasn't inclined to please, or conform to what anyone wanted these days, but she would try.

The administrator checked the early days of her youth — life before Gulag. Anastasia briefly described the life of the farming father, the shattered mother and the eight children born (but only five that lived). The maternal role passed to her as the eldest once the mother became saturated with sadness. How the girl's time was carved up so much she became fragile and translucent — stretched everywhere. Wash the mother and the children. Make the breakfast for four but feed seven. Sweep the cottage and steep the stinking wet bedding. Chase them to school and then trek to the fields. Cut, gather and tie until your hands were rough and raw, and start again that evening to make something from not nearly enough. She had relived it in her mind a thousand times in Gulag. In retrospect, easier times, maybe.

The administrator wondered, did Anastasia have friends at that time? A sweetheart perhaps?

Wearily she recounted, yes there were 'friends' — but they dissolved. A farm boy might have been sweet on her once, but it was fanciful, irrelevant.

Anya took a moment and considered this stout, dour, inanimate woman, and struggled to see any quality that may have endeared either friends or farm boys alike. Perhaps she was once?

She probed about that summer, when she was 15 years old — the prelude to Gulag. Anastasia described the aunt from the neighbouring area coming to stay in May 1963, following some unpleasantness in her marriage. Anastasia still toiled, but now she could frequent the crossroads on some longer evenings, with M and E and B. They were young she said, and silly, but harmless.

In her mind she saw them now — four girls sat on the dry wall; their high nellies propped up beside them and jeering the boys that passed by. When old men passed, their bicycles supporting them unsteadily following their card games, they giggled conspiratorially — whispering about the horror of being an old man's bride, and having to wash their undergarments. The horror! Occasionally, Mr M would take the bait and drop his bike, lurching towards them, stumbling. They'd fake screams and jump behind the wall; made safe by his limited sobriety and agility. She'd cycle home later, giddy with the sense of belonging and hope.

It wasn't always giddy. The aunt told them often that they were slovenly, ungodly and half wild. None wilder than Anastasia, the aunt said. She said this the day after Anastasia had come back from the field early and spotted the woman leaving the children's bedroom buttoning up her dress, with the father fixing his shirt behind her. Wildness was catching, it seemed to the girl.

A second aunt appeared on a Friday in July. Anastasia had no respect she said. Anastasia rolled her eyes and opined that the aunts had no respect for the poor mother. That earned a slap in the face. She ran. They roared after her that she might think she was special, but she needed some manners put on her. The bicycle flew down the lane.

Two came a week later, in a black car. She was summoned, and the father said that he had been wrong to stop school; he'd found her a school place, away from here. 'No', she said, panicking. She remembered the fear and the crowded room suffocating her and no one meeting her eyes. It was only a year and she'd be home at Christmas, Easter and in July he offered. 'No', she pleaded. He couldn't change it he said feebly. The mother never lifted her head off the pillow. A bag was already packed and they took her, one on each arm, and drove further south.

Anya said this must have been so difficult but the older woman just shrugged.

The Committee summoned them. All dressed in hues of grey. Introductions were made. Anastasia's posture was stiff as they explained how important they were, and what noble things the Government were doing to address the atrocities of the past. Anya was invited to proceed with the background of the case, which she did.

A very grey man asked Anastasia questions which she answered succinctly. The Committee asked the administrator to outline the time spent in Gulag; the hard labour undertaken by the applicant and any complaints. Anya tentatively read the notarised statement aloud. No governments liked to hear their own failings she thought, even if it was invited.

Twelve years labouring in the Gulag fields and in the laundry. Eight more years boiling laundry, tending pigs and making beads. Shorn hair. Bleeding cracked hands. Bleeding underneath, stemmed by rags. Hands bathed in toxic chemicals. Swollen bellies — with hunger or with child. Digging in frozen ground with raw hands and broken nails. Welts on ears from random clouts. Turned in eyelashes and rotten teeth. Ringworm and head lice. Pain and mauling and grunting from visiting old men, and from younger men in between work. Swollen knees and broken bones. A labyrinth of cold, unlit cells — to freeze in; or to bear children in; or to die in.

'Is this an accurate reflection of your experience madam?' asked the very grey woman. Anastasia nodded.

A grey man was clearly exasperated, 'I am quite surprised at your lack of animation throughout this hearing, and it is an issue madam. We see many witnesses. Their experiences have disturbed and distressed them, and the presentation of their case is impactful. It's concerning that we do not see much emotion and openness from you at all, given the list of grievances you have given?'

Anya panicked and her eyes darted, urging Anastasia to respond. Hoping she'd elaborate. Cry. Be more broken even.

Anastasia spoke, staring at Anya only, as if it was just those two.

'People must understand that being good, was very, very bad,' she said evenly. Every action had a consequence. The battered apples secreted for sickly inmates. The cabbage leaves hidden for mothers. Comforting hysterical arrivals, for everyone's sake. Hiding wet sheets and begging forgiveness from an unforgiving Superior. Any 'openness' was beaten shut, and no good ever came of Goodness.

She continued, 'As a young girl I was open and free. I committed no crime, yet I was imprisoned. Joy led to punishments and restrictions. Of both you and of those you might love. Being kind and free; dancing and singing, and flying on the handlebars of a bicycle on a July Saturday, meant your spirit would be grated into frozen ground and pummelled into wet ditches and smothered in the black of night. It meant ruptured ear drums or spleens or bellies. It meant you wished the worst on anyone else but yourself. It meant that weakness sickened you because it attracted more pain that you all had to bear witness to. It meant the Gulag.'

The very grey man dropped his pen to indicate he had heard enough. He spoke no more. The Committee adjourned. The called the women back a short time later.

The very grey woman spoke. 'Miss Duffy, it is clear that the labour and punishments applied were disproportionate to any perceived wrongdoing you or others may have committed. They were cruel, harsh and damaging, although you appear to be somewhat detached from that damage today.

'Detention in these settings was a practice of its time, but the state was unaware of the pain and suffering inflicted behind those walls. The role your family played in your incarceration is noted and the state cannot be responsible for that. Still, the state apologises for the pain and suffering that you have endured. We cannot change the past but merely ensure it does not reoccur. A compensation package for your labour and suffering will be assessed, based on your evidence today.

'However, for the purposes of accuracy in our notes, correspondence and any subsequent report, I would like to confirm that the place you only refer to as 'Gulag' is called St Josephs, and it was owned and ran by the Sisters of the Sacred Faith, located in Bawnmore, County Wexford.'

Anastasia stood to leave. Her last task of conformity was complete. It would always be Gulag. Even if it was the picturesque walled convent and laundry, on the hill, above the town.

If there had been phones
by Ann Seed

Shortlisted, Edinburgh Award for Flash Fiction 2022

Ripples, green with slime, raced across the water, slapping into the embankment before collapsing in the murk.

Her energy too was spent. The energy of hope, of keeping faith.

She turned from the window. The wind whistled through it, tormenting the flames crackling high in the fireplace.

There was a knock at the door.

'Come in,' she said.

'Phone call. Your cousin,' said the man.

His presence sent the usual shiver down her spine. But she kept her composure. She always did. Head high, she swept past him to the hall. There were no mobiles here... a landline or nothing.

'I am disheartened,' her cousin barked. 'You insist on undermining me.'

'False judgements,' said Mary quietly.

The stone walls echoed her words. A figure hovered in the shadows. Hard to keep confidences, to tether rabid tentacles worming into courtly ears, drip-feeding the poison of conspiracy.

'All these years, Mary. It can no longer be tolerated.'

Her cousin had the upper hand, held all the power. Mary held her breath. In recent days, she had almost prayed for what she knew was coming.

'Be ready in the morrow. Wear a simple gown.'

Mary thought she heard the hint of a quiver in her cousin's voice.

'I hope your God will treat you well, Elizabeth,' Mary whispered, clutching the cross around her neck.

Over the moat, the wind stilled. She dropped the receiver in its cradle, cutting off the call. At last she'd have peace.

The Unfinished Room
by Caoimhe O'Leary

Longlisted, Scottish Arts Club Short Story Competition 2022

She gently presses her baby finger against the magnolia wall. The kitchen is dry. The same colour extends to the hall and sitting room. Classic, simple, a little boring. Melissa has already arranged the furniture in the sitting room. A boxy television and VCR sit on a mahogany corner cabinet, the built-in press fastened with two brass knobs. A brown leather couch and two armchairs fill the space, and a warm Persian rug covers a significant portion of the wooden floor, a gift from overseas.

Moving down the hallway with its rich cream carpet, a luxurious choice for newly-weds, less sensible these days, Melissa surveys her work. The bathroom is acceptable, the avocado bath of its time and brightened with caricatures from a rare family holiday to France, camping. The master bedroom is pretty with a delicate floral print on the bedspread and curtains; the spare room is functional. The bedroom at the end of the corridor on the left-hand side is unfinished.

Two bicycles rest against the wall beside the back door. One is purple and one is pink, and both have silver tassels dangling from the handlebar.

'You taking particular care with this one?' Jacob lays his broad hand on Melissa's bony shoulder, peering in at the miniature house. 'A picky customer?'

'It's the house I grew up in,' Melissa says simply. She traces her index finger along the frame of the bikes, brushing her nail against the fluttering tassels.

'We loved cycling, my sister and me. We had our poor mother plagued as soon as there was a bit of a stretch in the evenings, and she'd let us cycle the four miles to and from school instead of waiting around for the childminder, who was always late.'

'I didn't know you have a sister.'

She has said too much. She can see that Jacob's eyes are alert, curious. It annoyed her, in the early days, his bumbling enthusiasm about her life. Melissa has fastened a shroud around herself, guarding her memories and she feels like Jacob is on the outside, probing her for more information.

'Had a sister.' Melissa stands up, wrapping her long arms around her thin frame. 'It's late,' she says. 'We'd better think about dinner.'

'Fancy take-out?' Jacob has accepted her bait. She hopes he won't ask her any more questions about the house, or her sister. He seems to have learned to hold his tongue over the years. Sometimes he forgets.

The house is different, different to her usual models. The all-American wrap-around porch, dining table for ten and two-car garage — most of Melissa's clients have big dreams for their kids. She has a bit of a formula for those dollhouses, ordering generic miniature furniture in bulk and kitting out replica houses, but tweaking things here and there to create some sense of individuality and originality, appeasing her clients' demands.

The scaled-down bungalow has a homely feel to it, she hopes. Melissa has taken care with the fittings — even the dresser in the kitchen has tiny crystal glasses and blue patterned china. She spent hours scouring the internet, sourcing a replica grandfather clock, the family heirloom. It looks out of place in the hallway, much as it did in real life, the girls' elbows and knees frequently black and blue from crashing into it as they played chasing down the corridor.

It is a little after midnight and Melissa cannot sleep. The room is hot. Jacob's hairy body and snores fill the bed. Melissa lifts Jacob's hand off her thigh, leaving a film of sweat behind. She swings her long legs out of the bed and pads downstairs in flimsy shorts and top, with a delicate faux-lace trim. Jacob bought them for her. She would prefer to cover her body in flannel pyjamas, buttoned to the neck. But it pleases Jacob when she wears them, and besides, anything heavier would be suffocating in the Arizona heat.

Light from the full moon floods in through the un-curtained window, illuminating the miniature house. Melissa slides open the sash, bringing in a waft of hot air, heavy with dust and sand. Jacob reminds her frequently that opening the windows is of little benefit. Using the air-conditioning is preferable, Jacob says. But she cannot stand the underlying hum of the machine and the corpse-cold feeling of the recycled air, a thousand breaths inhaled and spat back out, cleansed. Melissa longs for the cool dampness of air after a misty rain shower, the smell of wet grass.

Melissa creeps up to look at the miniature house in the moonlight. She pays little attention to the main body of the house. The bedroom. Something is not right in the unfinished bedroom. There is a dark smudge on the floor, spreading and spreading.

Melissa takes a cloth from her workbench, wets it, and rubs at the spot, rubs it and rubs it. She frowns, puzzled. She has done very little with this room and cannot think what could have spilled there. She turns on the light, her eyes startled in the sudden rush of brightness. There is nothing on the bedroom floor after all, a trick of the moonlight.

Masking tape X's crisscross the bare bedroom, marking where the scaled-down furniture should be positioned. Bunkbeds, a bedside locker with Melissa's reading lamp and a faded blue velvet chest overflowing with fancy dress-up clothes — Melissa knows where every item needs to be placed.

The walls of the bedroom are painted mint green, an unusual choice, Daisy's. Melissa had been sullen for days, only relenting when her mum whispered that as the grown-up of the pair, she could choose which of the new bunkbeds she would like. Top or bottom. Melissa avoids looking at the X spot where the bunkbeds should be, beside the window. Instead, she thinks about the other replica items which will need to be built and designed for the room.

A standalone doll's house. That will be tricky. A house within a house. Melissa imagines minuscule dolls, shrunk down to the size of ants, and the two girls, sisters, busying their lives with tea parties and fashion shows for the dolls.

'Lissa, Lissa,' Daisy whispered with a gentle lisp. 'Can my dolly borrow your dolly's yellow sparkly dress for the Grand Ball?'

'Balls are stupid, boring. My Barbies are going to a pool party in Ken's penthouse apartment.' There were times when the three-year age gap between the girls was more evident.

'So does that mean I can have the dress?' Daisy's face was hopeful.

Melissa thought about it for a moment and proposed a bargain. 'That dress is one of my absolute favourites. I'll only let you have a lend of it if you promise that you'll be really careful and only if I can have your Barbie car for the whole weekend. My Barbies want to arrive at the pool party in style. Oh, and I have booked out the whole dollhouse for Friday, Saturday and Sunday — it's a three-day party. You'll have to have your silly ball somewhere else.'

'Oh OK,' said Daisy. Melissa watched as Daisy's forehead wrinkled, and her lips parted slightly, crestfallen. Melissa imagined she could read Daisy's thoughts — Daisy envisioning her doll arriving in the golden dress, the belle of the ball, Prince Charming ready to greet her as she stepped out of the pink convertible car. Clodhopping up to a makeshift ballroom in the sandpit on the three-legged bald donkey wouldn't have quite the same appeal.

Melissa shivers in spite of the warmth of the room. The creak of the bed upstairs signifies Jacob is awake. He never moves in his sleep, stays sprawled in the same position all night, while Melissa tosses and turns frequently, her mind racing. She wonders what has woken him tonight.

She knows he will soon be down. He worries about her. Hurriedly she returns the cloth to its place on the workbench, stacks the miniature furniture up and is just about to click the light off and fill a glass of water in the kitchen when a bleary-eyed Jacob appears.

'Not able to sleep?' He rests his hands on her bare shoulders. 'What is it about this house?'

Melissa is folded into herself, arms crossed. She thinks of all the things she can never tell Jacob. He would leave her, surely he would leave her if he knew.

'Please Lissa, let go,' her sister's voice was tiny. Melissa caught her sister's legs and she swung them and swung them, as her sister held onto the ladder of the top bunk.

'It'll be fun,' Melissa had said, with a glint in her voice. 'You'll see.'

'Please Lissa.'

The miniature bunkbed is still wrapped up. The brown padded envelope is stapled shut, bubble wrap protecting the delicate wooden model. Melissa cannot open it, she cannot bear to look at it, to touch the top rung of the ladder which Daisy's slippy hands had held onto.

Melissa's hands had been frantic, trying to stop the slowly spreading red stain as it pooled around the base of the bunkbed, as if gathering together the blood would somehow make it all go away. She never meant to, oh Daisy, she never meant to...

Her parents eventually said it wasn't her fault. That it had been a tragic accident. That she was too young to know any different. That the childminder should have been keeping a better eye on the two girls.

But Melissa had been angry. Her swimming lesson cancelled, the teacher sick, Melissa waited twenty minutes in the rain for Laura, the childminder. Rivulets of water dripped from the ends of her plaited pigtails, and into her sodden school jumper, the smell of wet sheep. She left the house that blustery April morning without a coat.

Daisy had been home all afternoon with Laura. The more likely scenario, Melissa thinks, is that Daisy occupied herself all afternoon, while Laura took one of her long phone calls at the back door, pulling the cord of the house phone taut against the kitchen window and blowing exasperated plumes of smoke into the air.

Melissa's shoes squelched down the hallway. Daisy did not look up when Melissa entered the bedroom. She was lying belly-down on the top bunk, absorbed in her task. She had been left alone in the house, while Laura collected Melissa, a black mark which reluctantly emerged in the coroner's inquest.

Chunks and tufts of blonde Barbie hair lay in little piles on the floor. The doll's house was newly painted, garish colours slopped onto the walls and ceiling. Melissa's Barbie with the golden sparkling dress, the one her dad bought her as a present before he went working overseas, was propped up in the centre of the room. Her tightly bound plaits were unbound at last into a fuzzy halo, a purple bikini painted onto her body, and the golden dress cut into a sort of sarong, enhanced with downy dirty bird feathers.

'I thought you'd like it,' Daisy whispered. 'You said balls were stupid, so I decorated the house for the pool party.'

The dress, Melissa kept the tatters of the dress when she left behind the broken house at nineteen. America held promise, anonymity, an escape. Her father brooding in his usual spot, by the fireplace, the Persian rug long since frayed, the warm colours dulled and faded with dirt over time. Her mother, manic with activities, walking, walking, walking — anything to get out of that sad house.

Jacob's warm hand is still on her shoulder. She thinks of the golden dress, buried in her drawer under socks and underwear, the sad grey feathers wilted, the lustre lost from the threadbare garment. She could reach out, lay her fingers over his, lead him through each room of the miniature house, lay it all out bare for him. She lets out a weary sigh, breath she hadn't realised she was holding.

Still goin' strong
by Heather Finlayson

Longlisted, Edinburgh Award for Flash Fiction 2022

'This science and tech bit's not my thing, I'm off to check out the Egyptian section'.

'OK honey, see you in the café at one o'clock.'

Keith left to find the mummies. Dolly continued through the science section, fascinated.

'Hello, Dolly!'

She turned. The museum was empty.

'You're looking swell, Dolly.'

A hidden comedian. She had several friends who'd fit the bill. A stuffed sheep was mounted on a plinth nearby.

'I heard the Keith man call you Dolly. Fancy us having the same name!'.

She felt the room swayin' as she realised the source of the voice. Dolly the sheep appeared to be talking to her.

'They cloned me you know. I'm a scientific breakthrough, now I'm stuck here.'

Human Dolly was speechless, incredulous, utterly confused.

'Have you seen my lambs anywhere? Bonnie? The twins? The triplets?'

Tumbleweeds, then Dolly the sheep informed her, seemingly at random,

'I've learned a lot from living here. Loved the musicals exhibition! Genetic manipulation is awesome! The magic gallery is my favourite though'.

Her eyes darted. She must find someone. She relaxed a little, thinking it must surely be one of those telly gotchas.

Colours flashed in the air surrounding the pair.

Human Dolly found herself standing on the straw covered plinth, unable to move, horror reflected in her fixed stare, directed towards the now fully animated sheep.

'It's so nice to have you back where you belong!' sang the clone as she trotted off.

Beached
by Lorraine Queen

Longlisted, Edinburgh Award for Flash Fiction 2022

The waves crashed over the rotting carcass of the whale. Seaside was famous for its long sandy beaches and the tourists' dollars that it brought to the town were its most valuable income.

The dead whale must go! The town council held an emergency meeting and after several hours of debate and arguments, it was decided that the quickest way to dispose of the body was to blow it to smithereens. The small pieces would then disperse in the ocean and be carried away by the tides.

Councillor Smithers had once served in the United States Artillery Corps — just as a cook certainly, but a friend of his, Fingers O'Malley was still working as an explosives engineer at the mines a few miles away.

The following Thursday, the dignitaries of the town gathered on a hill where they could view the proceedings from a safe distance. Fingers — and they had been somewhat perturbed to see that his nickname referred to his lack of digits — had cleared the beach, and packed the the dead mammal with dynamite.

A siren sounded and the countdown began. Five, Four, three, two, one... Fire!

Eardrums popped at the mighty explosion and a red mist rose before their eyes. The corpse was indeed obliterated. Unfortunately, its entire remains now covered the beach. Also in the fallout were the hotels, shops and cafes on the seafront...

O'Malley slipped quietly out of town, glad that his fee had been paid in advance.

The Scottish Arts Trust Story Awards

www.scottishartstrust.org

The Scottish Arts Trust, established in 2014, supports the arts through voluntary action. The Trust provides platforms for showcasing the work of artists, writers, musicians and other arts practitioners, while also mobilising and drawing on the skills, energy and vision of volunteers committed to the creative arts.

Initiatives include awards, exhibitions, performances and publications in the visual and literary arts as well as contemporary music. The Trust aims to expand these opportunities by building on the experience of volunteers who seek a closer involvement with the arts. Currently, more than fifty volunteers located in six countries are involved in the operation of our projects.

From the outset, the Trust has benefitted from the support of the Scottish Arts Club in Edinburgh, Scotland. The Club was founded in 1873 by a group of artists and sculptors, including Sir John Steell, Sculptor to Queen Victoria, and Sir George Harvey, President of the Royal Scottish Academy. For twenty years they met in a series of premises around the West End of Edinburgh. In 1894, the building at 24 Rutland Square was purchased as a meeting place for men involved and interested in all arts disciplines. It was not until 1982, following contentious debate, that women were admitted as club members. In 1998, Mollie Marcellino became its first female President. Until her death in 2018, Mollie was also an avid reader for the Scottish Arts Club Short Story Competition.

The idea for the short story competition, which is open to writers worldwide, developed out of the Scottish Arts Club Writers Group. Alexander McCall Smith has long been a supporter and honorary member of the Scottish Arts Club, which has sometimes featured in his Scotland Street novels. He volunteered to be chief judge and remained in that role until 2020 when Andrew O'Hagan took over, followed by another long-standing honorary member of the club, Ian Rankin, in 2022.

Our chief judges are aided by a team of readers whose primary qualifications are a love of short fiction and a willingness to read, debate, defend and promote their favourites through successive rounds of the competition — a process that takes four or five months. In 2022, we established a Readers Register for volunteers around the world who would like to serve as readers for the writing awards.

Short story prize money has increased from a first prize of £300 in 2014 to £1,000 by 2017 and £3,000 from 2023. In 2017 we launched the Isobel Lodge Award, named after a dear member of the Scottish Arts Club Writers Group. This prize, which rose to £750 in 2020 is given to the top story entered in the competition by an unpublished writer born, living or studying in Scotland.

In 2018 we introduced the Edinburgh Award for Flash Fiction, with novelist Sandra Ireland as the chief judge. Sandra won the first of our short story competitions with her story, *The Desperation Game*, which lent its title to our first anthology. In 2021, celebrated authors Zoë Strachan and Louise Welsh took over as the flash fiction judges. In 2023, the flash fiction prize rose to £2,000 and the Golden Hare Award for the top flash fiction entry from Scotland to £500.

We enjoy celebrating the work of our short story finalists at the annual Story Awards Dinner held at the Scottish Arts Club — and the flash fiction writers at the highly entertaining Flash Bash.

The Scottish Arts Trust is a registered charity (number SC044753). All funds raised through our competitions are used to promote the arts in Scotland. Learn more about the programmes supported by the Scottish Arts Trust at www.scottishartstrust.org.

Acknowledgements

Our special thanks to international best-selling author, Ian Rankin, who took over as chief judge of the short story award in 2022 and to award-winning authors Zoë Strachan and Louise Welsh who continued as chief judges of the flash fiction award.

We are grateful to John Lodge whose donations support the Isobel Lodge Award, which brings such encouragement to many unpublished short story writers in Scotland. Thanks also to Sir Mark Jones whose support for the Golden Hare Award has helped to promote interest in the flash format across Scotland.

Our teams of dedicated readers reviewed and discussed over 1,500 entries to the short and flash fiction competitions in 2022. We are in awe of the energy and commitment the readers bring to successive rounds of these competitions and their passion as they make the case for the stories they love to progress through the competition.

We are indebted to Dai Lowe who works tirelessly as our story awards administrator, to Siobhán Coward who manages the short story readers and to Linda Grieg who does the same for the flash fiction teams. Our thanks also to Gordon Mitchell whose wonderful paintings give the story awards and our anthologies such a distinctive visual style. We are grateful to Amy Macrae for inspiring revisions to the story awards brand. On a personal level, I am thankful for the cheerful, meticulous and skilled professionalism of my co-editor, Claire Rocha.

Finally, a huge thank you to all the writers who have imagined, drafted, written, re-written and submitted stories in 2022. Your stories are packed with inspiration and creative passion. We look forward to reading more!

Sara Cameron McBean
Director, Scottish Arts Trust Story Awards
www.scottishartstrust.org